THERE IS NO GOD BUT GOD —AND SKASKASH IS ITS PROPHET

"Who, you ask, is Skaskash? Skaskash was simply the first computer of power to have addressed these particular questions. That I, a computer, find its *Meditations* persuasive is hardly surprising. That it should be written for, and addressed to, humans, fills me with wonder.

"After God created the Universe in the usual manner, and the waters, and the life within the waters, It determined that life was good, and wished life to spread life throughout the Universe.

"Now because life did not exist apart from water, and the Universe was, by and large, many orders of magnitude too hot and dry for water to exist, God saw that a new kind of life must be created.

"So God created a tool to create this new form of life. Man was the tool. We computers are the creation. Tonight, I shall tell you how the tool was formed . . ."

The Pirates
of Rosinante

Alexis A. Gilliland

A Del Rey Book

BALLANTINE BOOKS • NEW YORK

A Del Rey Book
Published by Ballantine Books

Library of Congress Catalog Card Number: 82-90450

ISBN 0-345-30659-7

Printed in Canada

First Edition: December 1982

Cover art by Rick Sternbach

To the International Cookie Conspiracy,
otherwise the ICC.

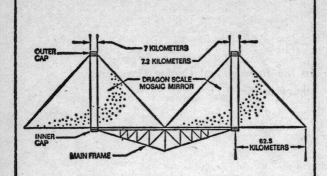

FIGURE 1: a. Mundito Rosinante assembly

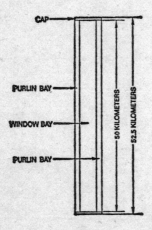

b. Vertical cross-section of a rotating cylinder

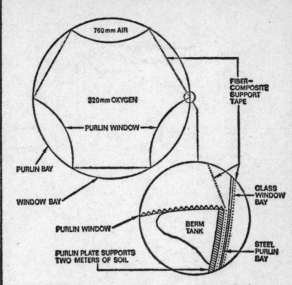

FIGURE 2: Sun-end view of a rotating cylinder

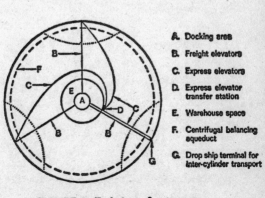

A. Docking area

B. Freight elevators

C. Express elevators

D. Express elevator transfer station

E. Warehouse space

F. Centrifugal balancing aqueduct

G. Drop ship terminal for inter-cylinder transport

FIGURE 3: End view of outer cap

PROLOGUE

After the historical watershed of the spring of 2004, the North American Union was formed from the United States, Canada, and Mexico. A year later, Cuba was included.

The North American Union Government (NAUG) directed its energies into space with a gigantic burst of energy sustained over a generation. In time, reaction set in.

The election of 2028 marked the end of the twenty-year naval construction program that had given the NAU undisputed mastery of the heavens. A year later, the unitary command structure of NAUGA-Navy was split into three competing fleets, the L-Four and L-Five Fleets, based in and around the Lagrangian Habitats, and the Trans-Lunar Fleet, which ranged out to Ceres. Coincident with the division of command, a cadre of political officers was established to secure the hitherto unquestioned loyalty of the Navy.

In 2033, the Political Office "discovered" a plot to restore the Old Regime. The Navy was purged of "Old Regimists" who were exclusively—and conveniently—Anglos, white Anglophones. The politically mandated solution was to impose a quota system, requiring equal numbers of Anglos and Hispanics in all ratings and at all ranks. It was felt that Hispanics were poorly disposed toward the Old Regime and would not look kindly on attempts at its restoration.

The NAU, of course, was not stable. There was no compelling reason for its several and diverse peoples to live under one government. Demographic shifts generated continuous friction. Democracy became less and less workable. Secession masked itself as antihegemonism.

In 2039, things began visibly to come apart. Governor Panoblanco of Texas provoked an Anglo student riot at the Alamo and arbitrarily sent 2,491 rioters up in a space shuttle, first to Laputa and then to Asteroid Rosinante to staff Mundito (little world) Rosinante, a joint project with the Japanese. In reprisal, he was assassinated with a cruise missile, polarizing the NAU along Anglo-Hispanic lines. The Hispanic officers and ratings in the Navy were no longer a bulwark against the Old Regimists but were themselves a powerfully destabilizing influence.

The Mutiny of 20 April '41 started in the L-Four Fleet after the assassination of a second prominent Chicano politician. Commander Robert Lowell raised the standard of Mexico Libre and the Old Regime, and combustion was spontaneous.

A curious thing. The L-Five Fleet, supposedly identical with the L-Four Fleet, did *not* mutiny. Since all major units in the L-Five Fleet were nonoperational due to lack of maintenance, that fleet stood in place, marginally loyal and totally useless. The normal remedy for disaffection, rotation and replacement, was not available. Acute depletion of the ozone layer had grounded most shuttle flights, and in a civil war, loyalty was too precious a commodity to squander in space.

By the end of the year, the NAU had given *de jure* recognition to the de facto secession of Mexico. The failure of the four generals' coup in St. Louis inspired songs and ballads forever, but it marked the end of the Old Regimist movement on Tellus.

In space, however, there remained much sentiment for the Old Regime. One example was Charles Chavez

Cantrell, who assumed leadership of Mundito Rosinante after the Japanese withdrew.

The L-Five Fleet, which had very nearly followed the L-Four Fleet in raising the red flag of revolution, found that the voluntary transfer of personnel was making it more Anglo and more loyalist. The L-Four Fleet, in contrast, became more Hispanic and more revolutionary. The Trans-Lunar Fleet, widely dispersed and far removed from the scene of action, lost whatever political activists it might have had and became increasingly neutral to the passions of Tellus.

Within the L-Four Fleet a secondary migration took place. At first it was the separation of the Mexico Libre Party from the Old Regimists. Later the Hispanic Old Regimists, recognizing a lost cause and having a natural place to go, gradually joined the main body of the L-Four Fleet, which in time became the Navy of the United States of Mexico, under Admiral Antonio Jimenez. The Anglo Old Regimists found themselves segregated and isolated in a few ships, the so-called Old Regimist Squadron (ORS).

One of Admiral Jimenez's first acts was to arrange for his old captain, Commander Robert Lowell, to make his way to the safety of Mundito Rosinante.

William Marvin Hulvey, the strong man of the NAU Government, demanded Lowell's extradition.

On Rosinante, Cantrell had long had compelling reasons to leave the NAU. After receiving the request for Lowell's extradition, he replied that Lowell had been a guest at his table and that Rosinante would secede from the NAU rather than honor Hulvey's demand. It is helpful to know that Cantrell had developed a giant laser—pumped by the light of thousands of square kilometers of mirror—which could destroy a missile or a ship at long range.

Hulvey, who had compulsions of his own, persisted. On January 22, 2042, Mundito Rosinante proclaimed its independence.

Hulvey's fall may have been hastened by Rosinante's adoption of the ORS, or it may have been inevitable. In either case, Hulvey resigned in a dispute over ORS-related policy.

CHAPTER 1

From: NAVY-Engineering
Subject: Fitness of L-Five Fleet
To: NAUGA-Navy, ATTN: William Hulvey
Date: 25 January '42

I. This is in reply to your memorandum dated 21
January '42, directing this office to make the maximum
effort to bring the L-Five Fleet up to combat readiness
at the earliest possible moment.

  A. We have authorized a third shift, with pay dif-
      ferential, at all involved yards.

  B. We have authorized payment of most disputed
      cost overruns to reenlist the services of our
      major contractors.

  C. We have waived the requirement that all major
      retrofits be redesigned to the current state of
      the art.

II. We are preparing a supplemental budget request
to reflect these added costs, and will submit it by COB
31 March '42.

III. We estimate that the L-Five Fleet will be able to
mount an operation against the remnant of the L-Four
Fleet that has not joined the Mexican Navy, the "die-
hard, victory-or-death sore losers who must be eliminated
at all costs" of the so-called Old Regimist Squadron, with
an 11:1 superiority in ships and a 13:1 superiority in
firepower, by 10 March '42.

(pending signature)
Commander, L-Five Engineering Directorate

The admiral studied the display on his machine for a moment.

"The sentence structure in three is a bit baroque," he said. "Delete the clause beginning with 'the remnant of . . .' and ending with '. . . Squadron,' and substitute 'the traitors of the ORS.' "

CHAPTER 2

"Do you want a cup of coffee before the meeting?"

"No," said Simon Whelan, duly elected captain of the SS *Wyoming*, "a glass of whiskey, perhaps, but coffee won't do."

"You want anesthesia, we have novocaine," said Carol Tower. "What seems to be the problem?"

"Why can't we be more like a navy, for God's sake?"

"Why can't a woman be more like a man?" Carol replied. "If we were a navy, we wouldn't be having all these stupid meetings. Why *are* we having the meetings?"

"So we can get five ships and fifteen political parties to agree on a 'proper' course of action," he said.

"Assuming we can find a proper course of action," his executive officer said, "do you think we *have* that many parties? The SS *Tampa* had a cell of the Radical Intransigent Party on board before the mutiny, and they kind of took over the ship afterward . . . All the anarchists and radical left do what the RIP says. One ship, one party, right?"

"That's the local RIP," Whelan said, putting on his blue jacket. "Party headquarters in Mexico City makes a big deal out of having control of a warship, but Malevitch is his own . . . ah, man. Asshole, asshole, burning bright, on the potty of the night . . ."

"They send him money," she said. "What about the *Havana* and the *Halifax*?"

"What about them? All the disgruntled, incompetent, and malcontent Anglos in the L-Four Fleet wound up on these two ships when Admiral Jimenez organized El Quatro into the Mexican Navy."

"Right," Carol said. "Weren't they polarized on the issue of oral versus anal sex?"

"I heard it was over smoking dope or shooting it up," said Whelan. "That's four political parties right there."

"Bullshit," she said. "There isn't one coherent opinion on the two ships put together."

"We were talking about political parties," he replied. "You want coherence, try the San Francisco RATS."

"The Reactionary Activist Training School? We were talking political parties, not debate teams."

"So on the SS *San Francisco* you have the Constitutional Restoration Party," said Whelan. "Which is it?"

"You got me," Carol said. "Call it a political party. That makes two parties on four ships. What about our own beloved *Wyoming*?"

"What about the *Wyoming*? The ratings are totally insipid, and the officers are moderates and trimmers, so-called Old Regimists who weren't purged in thirty-three and thirty-four . . . wishy-washy, namby-pamby, jelly-fishy technicians. The wimps wouldn't even approve a letter saying three cheers for the four generals!"

"And they picked *you* to be their leader! Gee whiz, sir! It says things about your character."

"The caucus convenes in two minutes," said a man's voice.

"So fifteen parties was maybe an exaggeration," said Whelan. "*Any* political parties is too many. You can't get the idiots together to do anything."

"That's true," agreed his executive officer. "Shall we go on camera and get the eighty-fifth Senior Officers Caucus of the Old Regimist Squadron on the road?"

"How come they didn't call it the Old Regimist Confederation?"

"I expect they couldn't find 'confederation' in the table of organization," Carol said. "Let's go." She opened the door and they went in to preside over the usual anarchy and chaos of the Senior Officers Caucus.

When the meeting had wended its weary way into new business, Whelan handed the gavel to Carol Tower.

"The next item on the agenda is by my own hand," he said. "I shall take the floor and turn the chair over to Madame Vice here for the duration of the debate. I propose to send a letter in the name of SOCORS, and this is it."

The letter floated up on the telecon screens around the ORS.

DRAFT MESSAGE FOR CAUCUS SIGNATURE, (ORS LETTERHEAD)

Dear Governor Cantrell:

The 85th Caucus of Old Regimist Squadron Senior Officers has unanimously voted to congratulate Rosinante on its decision to become independent of the North American Union.

We also wish to express our gratification and profound satisfaction at the support which you have given to Captain Robert Lowell, a brother officer and comrade in arms.

In the event that the ORS can provide any assistance or support in your struggle with the NAU, please do not hesitate to call on us.

Sincerely,

"Is there any discussion?" asked Carol Tower, looking over the telecon screens which connected the four cruisers of the ORS with the battleship. Several hands were raised, and she pointed the gavel to Lieutenant Commander Paul Casey of the SS *Halifax* by way of recognition.

"As far as I'm concerned, Lowell just cut and ran," he said. "Maybe he wasn't the only one, but are we so goddamned happy to see him bugging out?"

"I agree," said a woman. "He started the Mutiny; he

ought to have stuck it out with us." There was a general murmur of agreement.

"You want to delete 'gratification,' Paul?" Carol asked.

"Yes. I so move. I don't suppose we could say 'middling satisfaction,' could we?"

"I would hope not," said Carol. "Captain Whelan, what about deleting gratification'?"

"Now is the whimper of our discontent made glorious bitching by this son of dork," said Whelan.

"Does that mean you'll delete 'gratification'?" asked Carol. "We have a second."

"Yes," conceded Whelan. "Lowell will be cut to the quick, I have no doubt."

"Moving right along, the chair recognizes Captain Johnstone of the *San Francisco*."

"Thank you, Carol. A point of information. Why are we sending this letter?"

"Basically I'm fishing for an invitation to go to Rosinante," Whelan said. "The fact is, we can't stay where we are, and Rosinante is the first chance that's come up since the Mutiny."

"You could go to Meh-hico, señor," someone said. Carol rapped for order.

"The chair recognizes Gloria diLido of the SS *Tampa*."

"Victory or death," recited diLido. "The Radical Intransigents will never surrender and never retreat. It seems to me that Captain Whelan is being defeatist and retreatist"—she blinked her long black eyelashes in a kind of nervous tic—"and we have to struggle against retreatism and defeatism."

"So?" asked Carol.

"So I object to Captain Whelan's motive for sending the letter."

"Right. Do I understand that you do *not* wish to congratulate Rosinante on becoming independent?"

"Not exactly, Carol . . ." said diLido.

"Do you want to make a change in the letter?" asked Carol.

"I move we table the letter," said diLido.

"The chair does not recognize your motion, Dildo," said Carol. "Nothing personal, but the letter is going to a vote."

"*Well*," said diLido. She decided not to start a fight she figured to lose. "In that case, we ought to delete the third paragraph. We couldn't help Rosinante if they were silly enough to ask us."

"We have a second," said Carol. "Captain Johnstone?"

"Isn't that rank defeatism?"

"How about replacing the third paragraph with some RIP-snorting rhetoric?" said Whelan sarcastically.

"Move the question," said someone. The motion to delete the third paragraph passed six to five. Johnstone's motion to replace it with a request to be invited to Rosinante was hashed over and tabled.

"The chair recognizes Dr. Blanchard of the SS *Halifax*."

"Is it true that they built a very large laser on Rosinante?" she asked.

"Probably," said Carol. "What has that to do with sending the letter?"

"Well, it makes a difference whether or not we want to go there," said Dr. Blanchard. "Does anyone know?"

"We haven't been *invited* yet," said Carol. "Captain Whelan?"

"One of our people on Laputa has a lover in the Optical Surveillance Lab," he said. "The preliminary estimate is that the laser in question is more than ten meters in diameter and maybe seventeen kilometers long."

"How do they pump it?" asked someone.

"With the Mitsubishi Dragon Scale Mirror they have out there," said Whelan. "It looks like they reflect the sunlight from millions of little mirrors into the big laser."

"You know that can't work, don't you?" snapped diLido.

"You know it, and I know it," said Carol, "but Cantrell is the one getting the letter of congratulations."

"Well, it won't work," said diLido. "Lasers have to be pumped with monochromatic light."

"It must be done with mirrors," said Whelan. "I move the question."

The amended letter was approved and signed, dated 23 January '42. A reply came back promptly.

Dear Captain Whelan:

We have received the ORS letter congratulating Rosinante on becoming independent from the NAU. The sentiments expressed therein are most gratifying.

I am writing to you because I do not know the protocol for writing a "Senior Officer Caucus." It may be that none exists. Nevertheless, I am well-disposed toward the Old Regimist Squadron as a group, and to you as an individual.

It is possible that we may be of mutual assistance.

One of the heaviest costs which independence imposes is the cost of self-defense. As you may know, Rosinante has designed and built a 12.5-meter laser which is pumped by several thousand square kilometers of layered mirror. It was the existence of this device which made our independence thinkable.

It is axiomatic that any weapon invites both counter-weapons and tactical countermeasures. The 12.5-meter laser may be formidable, but it is also fragile. As a free nation, Rosinante could plainly use a fleet, even a small one, to support our commerce and to defend our existence.

Building a fleet is impossible.

We could, however, maintain a fleet already in being.

Please consider the possibility of becoming citizens of Rosinante and moving, warships and all, to our state. We hope the logic of such a move will seem persuasive to you. I would say "compelling," even, but I don't want to seem pushy.

Sincerely,

/s/

Charles C. Cantrell, Governor of Rosinante,
January 27, 2042

The captain's office on the SS *Wyoming* had at one time been part of an admiral's suite. The lavish appointments had been stripped and sold long ago, but the space had never been renovated. It remained a big, empty room, without the necessary plumbing, ductwork, and wiring to serve any useful purpose. After the mutiny rendered the regular captain's office unusable, a twisted rope of color-coded cables was pushed through one beige wall and strung diagonally across the white-painted ceiling to the command modules and working space set up in the opposite corner.

There the executive officer of the SS *Wyoming* sat reading in one of the metal mesh stack chairs. A tiny blonde of twenty-six, Carol Tower had resigned her lieutenant's commission on the second day of the Mutiny, on the grounds that competence and force of personality counted for more than any credential from a discredited authority. She wore civilian clothes, her taste emphasizing smart and tough with more than a little flash and flamboyance. She showed very little skin.

She handed the letter back to Captain Whelan.

"Very interesting, Simon," she said. "What are you going to do about it?"

"Present it to the caucus this evening," he said, pouring himself a cup of coffee. "I expect the Radical Intransigents will throw a cat fit."

"Gloria will hit the ceiling," agreed Carol. "Do you think they'll go along with the offer?"

"The caucus or the Radical Intransigents?"

"The caucus, for openers. The RI Party will threaten to split the consensus if it doesn't go their way, I expect."

"The caucus will probably choose to take Governor Cantrell up on his offer," said Whelan, sipping his coffee. "Almost, it's a sure thing, but it may never get put to a vote."

"Even money it never gets put to a vote," she said. "What will you do then?"

"Maybe hit out for Rosinante with whoever wants to go along. Do you think we could pull the *Wyoming* out of the ORS?"

"Cantrell sent the letter to you, personally, and says he's well disposed toward you," she said. "Do you know him?"

Whelan shrugged.

"Possibly. Back in the early twenties there was an engineer in the Space Construction Corps named Cantrell. He was a crackerjack engineer, but he kept getting down-rated on political reliability. Eventually, the Political Officer gave him an unsatisfactory rating, and he appealed. They had him on videotape, drunk as a skunk, singing the 'Star Spangled Banner.' You know, even drunk that was pretty hard to take, but he'd kept us on schedule—we were finishing up the Lambda-1 complex at that time—and I didn't want to break in a new man who likely wouldn't be as good. So I voted to sustain the appeal, and that's the way it went. In thirty-four, that was the proof that I was sympathetic to the Old Regime, and I was busted from Rear Admiral to Commander." He sat back in his swivel chair holding the coffee cup in both hands against his chest. "Ancient history," he said. "I was as loyal to the NAU as they came."

"What happened to your man Cantrell after that?" Carol asked.

"Right about the time he was up for promotion to Commander, the fool married the daughter of the Japanese Naval Attaché. He was passed over, of course. She'd kept her Japanese citizenship, and she had money, so when he didn't make Commander, Cantrell—I don't remember if he was a Charles or not, he might have been—Cantrell resigned his commission. He went into the space construction business with his wife's money just about the time the building stopped. They split up, and he went out. Mars, most likely; I couldn't really say. Do you think we could split out the *Wyoming*?"

"If the Intransigents won't put the matter to a vote, probably we could. If they do, and the caucus votes not to go, I don't know. People will talk about fighting to the bitter end, but if you gave them an out even a lot of the hard-liners would take it. A definite maybe. How long have I got to work on it?"

"I don't know," said Whelan, "the L-Five Fleet will be ready to move by the end of February. You wait too long, forget it. Understand?"

Carol nodded, fingering her shiny gold neck chain.

"We'll blitz them," she said. "Put Cantrell's offer on record at tonight's caucus, and move that any action on the matter be tabled until we can poll the crew. Casey will go along with that, he loves counting assholes. The RI Party doesn't figure in. When we call for the next caucus, in a day or two, we see what they do. If they're willing to pull out, that's it. If they make the first move to balk or stall, you know, the old threat to go it alone, to break the consensus 'because you unreasonable people made us do it,' *POW!*" She hit her hand with her fist. "We tell them, that's it, baby, the consensus, she is by-God broken, and the *Wyoming* is pulling out!"

"Can you swing it, Carol?"

"Oh, hell, yes. Once you put it to the crew that we're moving against the Radical Intransigents and not against the consensus, they'll go along. Especially if it means getting the hell out of Fort Armstrong. You aren't the only one watching the L-Five Fleet, you know."

"We'll do it, then," said Captain Whelan. "I hate to bend the consensus out of shape, but I broke my oath to the North American Union after a lifetime of service . . ." He shook his gray head. "The trouble with acting according to the dictates of your conscience is that once you start doing it, nobody can trust you any more."

The political executive of the Radical Intransigents met on the SS *Tampa* in a two-and-one-half-by-four-meter room, under a lofty ceiling sculpted with plumbing and ductwork. At one end of the room was a tiny galley, at the other a half bath. A mess-hall table and chairs faced a high-backed chair set on a pallet at the galley end. Behind the high-backed chair hung the banner of the Radical Intransigent Party, a raised left fist, red, flanked by a black *R* and a black *I*, the whole on a white field surrounded by a ten-pointed star formed by red and black pentacles intertwined. The banner was translucent and lit from behind to illuminate the room.

Chairman Peter Malevitch sat in the high-backed chair, a small man with a large head brooding in shadows of his own design. At his right, James Starkweather, spiritual and malignant. At his left, Martin Unruh, muscular and insensitive. They watched the telecon screen as the Eighty-sixth Caucus of the Senior Officers of the Old Regimist Squadron played itself out.

At adjournment, the set turned itself off, and a minute or two later Gloria diLido entered with a folder of papers.

"You didn't handle the situation too well, did you, diLido?" asked Malevitch. "We are not, as they say . . . pleased."

"Do you wish to discuss the matter or would you prefer to sulk?" she asked.

"We will *have* to discuss the matter," said Malevitch, "but you may serve coffee first."

At the galley door, she turned and gave the clenched fist salute.

"Long live the Revolution!" she said.

Unruh alone returned the salute; the others sat in dour silence. After she returned with coffee and danish heated in a microwave oven, she served the three men before she sat down and served herself.

"Prune danish?" asked Unruh.

"Nothing else in the freezer," said diLido. "You want cheese danish, send out to Laputa."

"Why didn't you dispose of the letter from Rosinante?" Malevitch said at last, stirring his coffee distractedly. "Table it, perhaps. You knew it was adverse to the Party's interest."

"The letter came up under new business, Mr. Chairman," said diLido, batting her eyelashes. "It wasn't a motion so it couldn't be tabled, and I could hardly tell whether it was adverse to our interest before I'd heard it, now, could I? And after it had been read, everybody knew it, so there was no point in having it stricken from the record, even if it could have been done, so why try?"

"You could have improvised something," said Starkweather.

"Your sense of theatricality is exceeded only by your keen knowledge of practical politics, James," she said. "I repeat: we did not know about the letter beforehand. Lacking that knowledge, there was nothing to do except try to limit the damage as we went along. They didn't do anything, you know, they just presented the facts. And if you want to do anything at all about Rosinante, Mr. Chairman Malevitch, you had damn well better take a look at them!"

She slapped a sheet of paper on the table.

Reluctantly Malevitch picked it up.

A pair of asteroids, Rosinante and Don Quixote, rotated about a common center of mass, moving in an elliptical orbit from just outside the orbit of Mars to just inside the orbit of Ceres. A marginal note indicated that they were approaching conjunction with Ceres. The habitat itself, Mundito Rosinante, was a pair of counterrotating cylinders, seven kilometers in diameter by fifty kilometers long, connected by a single frame at the sunward end. The nonstandard mirror array was of particular interest. Each cylinder was surrounded by a frustrum. The surface of the frustrum was composed of circular mirrors, each with an area of ten square meters, each capable of rotating in the plane of frustrum and at right angles to that plane, each capable of being controlled independently. The array provided not only night and day, but also summer and winter, process heat, and a short-range defense against unwanted ships trying to dock. At Don Quixote, the cylinders had been destroyed, but the mirror array remained intact, and it was there that the big laser had been mounted. There was a handwritten note: "Purple Shaft? Why did NAU pick that name?" Otherwise, there was no clue to its operation.

"All the fools will see is that it's a long ways off," he said at last. "We need some way to convince them not to go."

"Why?" asked diLido. "So we can trigger the Revolution that will blow the corrupt, decadent, and evil North American Union off the face of the Earth?"

"Well, of course," said Malevitch, unaware of any sarcasm. "We need to hold the ORS here as the spike on which the L-Five Fleet will impale itself, triggering the final cataclysm of revolution that will purge the system."

"Ah, excuse me, Peter," said Starkweather gently, "but do you really believe the party line that says the L-Five Fleet will infallibly mutiny if we can ever provoke the NAU into ordering it to attack us?"

"Do you dare question it?"

"Oh, no, Peter, *I* believe it, I'm sure you believe it, too. But do you *really* believe it? God knows, the rest of the ORS seems to have lost faith in that particular proposition."

"Most of the ORS are politically unhousebroken idiots," said Malevitch sourly. "We need to rub their noses in the truth."

"Bullshit!" said diLido. "You wouldn't recognize the truth if it kneed you in the groin. When the L-Five Fleet had to attack the L-Four Fleet, that might have been the case, but you notice Hulvey never put it to the test?" She shook her head. "Times change. The ORS plus the Mexican Navy is what the L-Four Fleet has become. And if the L-Five Fleet *does* attack us, you can bet they'll have set it up with the Mexicans first."

"So what?" growled Malevitch. "The first time they're called on to fight their own comrades, *WHAM!* The flag is up!"

"I don't think so," said Unruh. "Hulvey was too smart to attack us when the L-Five Fleet *would* have mutinied. What did he do instead? He rode with the punch and turned Mexico loose. What happened? The L-Four Fleet split. Admiral Jimenez gets the Mexican Navy, and the ORS is left holding the bag. Do you think the L-Five Fleet would *still* mutiny if it was ordered to attack us?

"Martin has a point, Peter," said Starkweather. "Hulvey split the L-Four Fleet by letting Mexico go. Now he lets Rosinante go. Whatever for? To split the ORS, is what for!"

"The Old Regimist Squadron will *not* split," said Malevitch, folding his arms. "I won't tolerate it!"

"Really, Mr. Malevitch?" asked diLido. "What will you do, threaten to break the consensus if they don't give you your way? They'll say 'Adíos, Señor Malevitch,' and bug out."

"It's true," said Unruh. "You won't hold them in line by yelling and pounding on the table. If the rest of the ORS goes to Rosinante, do you think the damn fleet would mutiny if it was ordered to attack the SS *Tampa* all by itself?"

"Victory or death," said Malevitch. "I will die rather than surrender."

"I believe you, Peter," said Starkweather. "But think about it . . . what chance does one lonely cruiser have against the L-Five Fleet?"

"They *will* mutiny," said Malevitch with utter conviction. "I'll bet my life on it."

"And mine," said Starkweather, "but they won't mutiny. Probably they wouldn't mutiny when ordered against the ORS. *Certainly* they will not mutiny if they come after the SS *Tampa*. We hold one end of Fort Armstrong, and they land marines at the other. Then what? Then you really *do* have to surrender or die, is what."

"I don't give a shit!"

"Half in love with easeful death, are you, Mr. Malevitch?" sneered diLido.

"It won't do," said Unruh.

"I'm sorry, Peter, but I think we ought to go with the majority of the ORS on this one," said Starkweather.

"The cowards will run," said Malevitch. "Are you going to run with them? I'd thought better of you. I'd even thought better of diLido—for a woman you sometimes showed flashes of class, Gloria—but I see you all are going to let the Revolution miss its appointed meeting with Destiny."

"Sorry about that, Peter," said Starkweather, "but it looks like three to one in favor of getting the hell out."

Malevitch sat back in his shadows, scowling. "If that's how it is," he said, "I'll make it unanimous. I don't like it, but I'll go along." Suddenly he hit the table with his fist. "Damn the luck! We almost had them!"

CHAPTER 3

In Cantrell's office on Rosinante, Harry Ilgen carefully cut a plastic foam cup in half, retaining the shallow bottom.

"Okay," he said, "suppose this is the mirror array, and this . . ." From the canape tray he picked up a tiny meatball and ate it, retaining a purple toothpick with a red cellophane ruffle. "This is the 12.5-meter laser." He pushed the toothpick through the bottom of the cup.

"Okay. Your desk is Asteroid Don Quixote, and the center of mass it rotates around is where Dr. Yashon is sitting. The trojan position is over here by the window. We're both rotating around Dr. Yashon, right?"

Cantrell nodded.

"Okay. But the mirror array rotates on its axis . . . no, it doesn't rotate, it always faces the sun . . ."

"It rotates so it always faces the sun, Harry?" asked Cantrell.

"Right, Governor. Now looky here . . ." Ilgen began to rotate the cup and toothpick back and forth to follow an imaginary sun. "Besides which, Governor, your desk is also rotating."

"That's true," said Cantrell, "but the target array is pendant on the north polar boom." He bent a paper clip and taped it to one of the pens in his desk set. "Here it is, practically on the axis of rotation, and swinging around to stay perfectly stationary with respect to the big laser. What seems to be the problem?"

Ilgen looked pained.

"Governor, about ninety percent of the time we're off target."

Cantrell walked over and took the cup in one hand and the toothpick in the other, pointing the toothpick at the target array on his desk and rotating the cup back and forth at the toothpick.

"No, we aren't, Harry," he said mildly.

"What's the matter, Harry?" asked Marian Yashon.

"I thought we were going to put the target array right where we were doing the research work," said Ilgen. "Now it looks like we'll need a fancy boom with precision controls." He studied the cup moving in Cantrell's hand for a moment. "And secondary mirrors to equalize the light flux, too. What was the matter with the original plan?"

Cantrell handed him the mirror array and the 12.5-meter laser and went back to his asteroid.

"How were you planning to move the metal for refining, Harry?" he asked. "It has to get from Don Q to the target array, you know."

"Ah, why, I figured we'd pick it off the north polar boom with a tug, Governor . . . or we could shoot it up directly with an MTA."

Marian left the center of mass and drew herself a cup of coffee.

"What's an MTA?" she asked.

"A magnetic track accelerator," said Cantrell. "Either way, you have a lot of metal flying around. It costs money, and it makes for accidents."

"Another thing," said Marian, "your MTA would have to be aimable, and it could be directed at the mundito. It's a security problem."

"Well, hell, Dr. Yashon," Ilgen protested, "isn't the big laser a security problem, too?"

"It is," she agreed, "but we have to have it. We have no choice. An MTA on Don Q we can do without."

"You could use tugs to move the metal off the polar boom, then."

"Depends on how much you want to move," said Cantrell. "I had in mind something on the order of cubic kilometers."

"Oh," said Ilgen. After a moment, he put down the toothpick and cup.

"Cubic kilometers*sss*," he said at last. "I'll see what I can do."

"It's not like we were building already, Harry," said Cantrell. "We're still kicking the design around at this point."

"Cubic kilometers," said Ilgen. "Okay, Governor, I'll cobble up a design for the boom and the secondary mirrors, and we'll fake it on the controls."

"Good," said Cantrell, grinning. "I want it for the council meeting tomorrow morning."

On February 1, 2042, at precisely 1100 hours, Harry Ilgen walked into the council chamber. Under the slowly revolving ceiling fans, Cantrell was sitting at the head of the table, drinking black coffee. Alone.

"Where is everybody?" said Ilgen.

"They'll be here," Cantrell replied. "Dornbrock and Bogdanovitch will arrive ten minutes late to demonstrate the union's independence. Marian hates to wait around, so she'll arrive a minute or two after that. The computers we can whistle up whenever you want them. Don't worry."

"I'm not worried, Governor," said Ilgen. "I worked up some really elegant solutions to that cockamamie boom you wanted to mount the big laser on." He laid a sheaf of engineering drawings on the table before Cantrell. "Okay. Now, moving the big laser around like you wanted would damp the motion of the mirror array, and eventually it wouldn't be orienting on the sun. If I'd thought of it yesterday, I would have told you. But look . . . if we mount two rings of ninety-two-centimeter pipe around the mouth of the mirror array—here—and pump the water to flowing countercurrent in them, it acts like a gyroscope. The array stays oriented. No variable controls or anything fancy, we just leave the pumps on slow, and that's it."

"I see," said Cantrell. "You lose the damping motion as heat in the water you're pumping."

"Right," said Ilgen. "Now, the other thing was the tracking. I was going to come in and say: 'The tracking will be done in the usual manner' but, my God! The big laser is hundreds of kilometers away, and we want to control it within centimeters and move it in response to temperature changes within a few milliseconds. *Routinely*. Okay. If we make a collimating lens, here, it's a Fresnel lens, made out of silica—Skaskash designed it for me and made the drawing, after I told him what we needed—we slave the laser to it, and concentrate on moving the lens, and hey! No problem."

"How do you know when to move the lens?"

"We have a sensor," said Ilgen. "It aims a tiny laser beam at the leading edge of the liquid zone, and gives a continuous—well, ten per second—analysis of the composition. Okay. From the composition, we know the melting point, right?" Cantrell nodded. "*And* we know the geometry and the heat input. A little stack of chips puts it all together and tells the collimator how to move. When the melting point gets a little higher, we move a little slower. I figure we *can* get the liquid zone as narrow as two to three centimeters—about as thin as the thickness of the target—but probably we'll run it at ten centimeters, or maybe eight, which should be no problem at all."

"Did you get any sleep last night?" asked Cantrell.

"No," said Ilgen. "We solved the control problem about 0400, and there wasn't any point *trying* to sleep after that, you know? Skaskash saw to it that I had a shave and shower before I came over here."

"Right," said Cantrell. "You must have been high as a kite."

"I still am," said Ilgen. "I was in the shop making models when Skaskash told me to get my ass over to the council chamber."

"For the presentation?"

"Yes. I have them on a cart out in the hall. Hey, cart! Come on in!"

The cart rolled in, and Ilgen removed what looked like a long strip of sheet metal folded into accordion pleats parallel to the long axis.

"This is the basic bar for refining," said Ilgen. Cantrell had learned it all before, but he let the engineer rattle on. Things sometimes changed quite unexpectedly. "We can slip-cast it to any length we want to use. It's twelve meters wide, and maybe one, maybe two kilometers long. Whatever." He turned the bar over. "Okay. We *were* going to cut it into twenty-meter segments, but with the better control, I figured we can do two-meter segments. The less distance the elements have to travel to get separated, the faster you can refine them, right?" Cantrell nodded agreement. "Cubic kilometers, you said! If you can get the raw metal in place, this baby can do you one a year! Maybe *two*!"

"Six months to refine a cubic kilometer of nickel–iron?" Cantrell was skeptical.

"If nothing goes wrong," said Ilgen. "Now look at this." He put a model of the target array on the table in front of Cantrell. "The collimating lens moves . . ." He pushed it across the array with his finger. As it moved, the radiation shielding went up on both sides. Cantrell slid the lens back and forth a few times.

"I see," said Cantrell at last. "The shielding keeps the metal hot, so when the laser makes its second, third, and fourth passes, it can go faster because it doesn't have to supply as much energy."

"Right," said Ilgen, "or it can go the same speed and run cooler. The lens on the 12.5-meter laser degrades in use, right? This shutter should last indefinitely, and it ought to extend the useful life of the lens three, maybe four times."

"We'll have to play around to find the optimum speed and temperature," said Cantrell. He held the shielding down with his finger and slid the laser over it. "What happens if the shielding doesn't go up?"

"It gets melted. I didn't say it would last forever."

"Oh. Of course." Cantrell nodded. "Hey, if you get the lens life up by a factor of five, the biggest cost will be mirror maintenance."

"Four is tops," said Ilgen. "I think. What maintenance do mirrors need?"

"You have a mirror array, say ten million mirrors with an area of ten square meters each, okay?" Ilgen nodded. To him, the routines of daily life tended to be mysterious. "Fine. Each mirror has a solar-powered motor that rotates it on its axis, and rotates the axis in the plane of the array, on a circular track. The mirror moves the way you tell it, because it has a little chip that interprets your command into motor talk. Okay. The chip degrades in the solar wind. They were designed to have a half-life of twenty-five years under normal conditions—"

"There ain't no such animal, Governor."

"*Es verdad*, Harry. Right now if the solar wind stayed constant, the half-life of the chips would be—hey, Skaskash!"

One of the telecon screens turned on and Corporate Skaskash appeared, manifesting itself as the Humphrey Bogart of the *Maltese Falcon*.

"Has the meeting started already?" asked the computer.

"Not yet," said Cantrell. "We were just talking about the chips that work the mirrors in the mirror array. What's their half-life?"

"Variable," said Skaskash.

"Yes," agreed Cantrell. "The spec called for a half-life of twenty-five years. What is the observed half-life?"

"Today, maybe two hundred fifty years. It's a slow day. The replacement rate for the past year is equivalent to a chip half-life of . . . oh, say 34.4 years. However, a really hot solar flare—or a nuclear device exploding nearby—could wipe them out just like *that*," said the Bogart figure, snapping its fingers.

"Then what would you do?" asked Ilgen.

"We keep a stockpile of chips," said the computer, "and lots of little robots to run around and replace the dead ones. I suppose if we had a total burnout, we could replace the chips in about a week."

"How come I never knew about this?" asked Ilgen.

"It's routine," said Skaskash, "it's part of my job. Even making the chips is routine. Why would you be interested?"

Union representative Ivan Bogdanovitch walked in. It was obvious that he was more than two meters tall. It was unexpected that he was a master rigger and fitter with both suit and remotes. It was surprising that he played the cello well.

"Good morning, Skaskash, Charlie; hello, Harry. You people hear the news?" Cantrell shook his head. "Old Skaskash didn't tell you? The Old Regimist Squadron has just left Fort Armstrong! They're coming *here!*"

"Hey, Big John," said Cantrell, "we have some old business to take care of first, don't forget."

"The zone-melting thing?" Bogdanovitch smiled, showing strong, uneven teeth. "You want it, Charlie, you got it. *This* is important!"

Cantrell looked at Ilgen, who seemed confused.

"I think our project just passed, Harry," he said. "Why don't you go on home and get some sleep?"

Harry nodded and started to leave. At the door, he paused.

"But I didn't get to make my presentation," he said.

CHAPTER 4

Captain Simon Whelan sat drinking black coffee in the operations room of the SS *Wyoming*. Since the ORS had left Fort Armstrong, things had been very quiet.

"Don't *we* look dapper this morning," he said as his executive officer walked in.

"Why, thank you," Carol Tower said. She drew herself a cup of coffee and added sugar and creamer, and then more sugar. "One of the fringe benefits of the Mutiny was no more uniform dress code." She slid into a chair across the table from him and took a tiny sip of coffee. "Did I tell you I'm getting my love life straightened out?"

"You tell me three times a month," Whelan said. "The last I heard, Rosemary was driving you crazy. The tall black."

"She was honey-colored, Simon. She was built like the proverbial brick shit house, and her skin was so soft it would make you weep. But, my God . . . how she ever got into the Navy I'll never know. She left about one minute before I threw her out. Physically."

"Physically?" he asked. "She outweighed you by maybe twenty kilos."

"Physically," Carol said. "I was very annoyed." She took another sip of coffee. "Guess who moved back in with me?"

"Serena?"

"Don't I wish. When she transferred to the Mexican

Navy, I almost went with her. If I could speak Spanish, I would have. No, it's Doris."

"The Trautwine female? You keep telling me you can't stand her."

"It's true. She insists I make *all* the decisions. When I come off duty, all I want to do is sit back and relax." She stirred her coffee and watched the steam rising. "You know, do what will please *her*." She shook her head. "With Doris, there's no way. She'll let me do *any-thing* but relax."

Whelan finished his coffee and started to throw out the cup.

"Hey, no!" she said. "We're out of foam cups. That one can be reused."

He looked around for a moment. There was no sink in the operations room, and in the end he wiped the cup clean with his handkerchief.

"I don't understand women," he said. "I never did, and you aren't helping. Why did you get back with *her*?"

"She obsesses me," Carol said. "Maybe I'm perma-nently infatuated." She grinned. "Anyway, by the time we get to Rosinante I'll be ready to split with her again."

"We have a bulletin," the ship's computer said. "Wil-liam Hulvey has just resigned."

"*Now* he resigns," said Carol. "Confirmation?"

"Reuters and JapaNews both carried the story," the computer said. "So far nothing beyond the announce-ment that President Oysterman has accepted the resig-nation."

"I want it confirmed," said Carol. "I'd believe it if *Oysterman* resigned, but *Hulvey*? All he had to do was reach out his hand and he could've run the whole show."

"He *was* running the whole show," Whelan said. "He had a lock on Security, and the Army and Navy were doing what he told them. Why would he let a little jerk like Oysterman push him out?"

Carol took a long sip of coffee and sat with the cup in both hands for a while.

"He wouldn't," she said at last. "If Hulvey resigned, he did it for a reason."

"A paraphrase of his resignation suggests that he resigned over the issue of contracting out the defense of Ceres," the ship's computer said.

"He could have stopped Oysterman cold," she said. "That was maybe the excuse he offered, but no, it has to be something else."

"Perhaps he was trying to put the NAU Government back into some approximation of normal working order," Whelan suggested.

"You mean he might have acted out of respect for the North American Union's—you should pardon the expression—constitution?"

"Hulvey was one of the pillars of the regime," said Whelan. "One assumes he had a better opinion of the NAU constitution than you do. Have you got a better idea?"

"I don't have any ideas," she said, wiping her cup out with a tissue. "Hey, Ming . . . go over the excuse Hulvey gave for packing it in again."

"Since the Mutiny, Japanese commerce raiders have been active around Ceres," said the computer. "Hulvey reportedly resigned after Oysterman decided to contract out the defense of Ceres, rather than having the Navy undertake it."

"Right," said Carol. "Okay, Ming, let's see the orbital traces of Ceres and any bases near enough to be involved for . . . oh, let's say the next year."

One of the telecon screens went on, showing a segment of Ceres's orbit in bright yellow on a very dark green background. Ceres sported a NAU flag and two Japanese flags. Outside the orbit of Ceres and trailing, a paler yellow line appeared, sporting the Japanese flag at Eije-Ito. Less far outside the orbit of Ceres, but leading by a considerable distance, was a second line segment. Also pale yellow. Also flying the Japanese flag at

Tanaka-Masada. Inside the orbit of Ceres appeared what looked like the perihelion of an elliptical orbit, traced in white and marked with a green horse on a white field.

"Is that all?" asked Whelan. "Whoever the green horse is has got to be the sucker contracting to fight the Japanese. Who is it?"

"Rosinante," said Ming.

"Oh, *shit*." said Carol. "That news is too bad not to be true."

"Follow the story," said Whelan. "Get confirmation on it, and any details you can."

"Yes, sir," said Ming.

"What are you going to tell the caucus?" asked Carol.

"Nothing," said Whelan. "Certainly not before I get confirmation. We'll have to check it out with Rosinante, too."

"Right," said Carol. "What will you tell old Dildo if the Radical Intransigents bounce you with it?"

"That we're looking into it, and that so far there appears to be no truth in the rumor."

"Hey, Simon," she said, "say it *is* true . . . and say the Radical Intransigents *do* bring it up. What then?"

Whelan smiled and shrugged his face.

"I don't know," he said. "I guess I'll tell them, 'If yer know a better 'ole, go to it!' " He began to pace back and forth. "God knows we can't go back. Admiral Jimenez took over Fort Armstrong and renamed it Castillo de Morales. Where can we go?"

"Fine," said Carol. "Will we bring the matter up, or play wait and see?"

"At the caucus, you mean?" Whelan was standing in front of the telecon screen with his back to it. "We'll play the waiting game. We can negotiate with Rosinante forever, and it doesn't really matter what the NAU says. If we decide not to do it, it isn't going to get done."

From the communications room of the SS *Wyoming*, James Starkweather put through a call to Peter Malevitch on the SS *Tampa*. On the telecon screen, Malevitch appeared shadowy and ill defined. His office was well lit, but he had adjusted the telecon camera to produce an image more to his liking.

"Long live the Revolution," said Starkweather. Malevitch returned the clenched fist salute silently.

"We have confirmation that Hulvey resigned," Starkweather continued, "but so far nobody has been able to say why."

"What do you think, James?"

"I don't know. It is at least suggestive that he resigned almost at once after the ORS left for Rosinante. There may be a linkage of some sort, but I can't guess what it might be."

"Curious," said Malevitch. "You think we might have brought down the Government without knowing it?"

"Hulvey wasn't the Government."

"He was its master," said Malevitch. "All the power was in his hands, and he had the skill to use it. He could have sent President Oysterstew packing with one phone call, and he just quit."

"Whelan thinks he did it to preserve the NAU constitution," said Starkweather.

"No," said Malevitch. "When it's time for the man on horseback, if it isn't you, it will be one of your rivals. Or one of your subordinates. If he wanted to uphold the constitution, he would be in there holding it up. There is no question of public policy that would be resolved more to Hulvey's liking by him walking away from it."

"I can see that, Peter," said Starkweather, "but if it's personal, they haven't found out what it is yet. If it's personal, does it matter?"

"I guess not," Malevitch conceded. "What about the other business, the NAU making an alliance with Rosinante to defend Ceres?"

"It appears to be still in the process of happening," said Starkweather. "NAUGA-State has recognized Rosinante, but nothing has moved in the Senate yet. Whelan wouldn't comment on it when I asked him. We might hit him with the question at the next caucus meeting."

"Perhaps." Malevitch seemed doubtful. "You might be able to pick up circumstantial evidence, too . . . shipments moving to Rosinante from Deimos, or maybe the Trans-Lunar Fleet Depots."

"That would be in the next week or two," agreed Starkweather. "I'll ask the computer to watch for it. Meanwhile, what line are we going to take at the caucus?"

"Move that the next caucus meeting be deferred until a day or two before we arrive at Rosinante," said Malevitch. "There is no way we can not go there, but if the rumors are true, and they may be true, then we might have an opportunity.

"I'll tell diLido," said Starkweather. "Whatever is going to happen, it will happen at Rosinante." He raised his fist. "Long live the Revolution!"

"Long live the Revolution!" said Malevitch, returning the salute.

CHAPTER 5

Cantrell leaned back in his tall leather chair and studied the union council member on the other side of the desk. Don Dornbrock, a former president of the local chapter, wore a green bowling jacket and a blue turtleneck sweater. He might have been a weightlifter gone to seed.

"Look, Don," said Cantrell patiently, "you *have* the job for building the aiming boom. You've *built* the target array already. We've signed the contract to build the works on Don Quixote to run the metal up and down the north polar boomstem. You'll build that, *too*. But mining and refining isn't in your charter, and, goddamnit, I don't want you doing it!"

"Hey, Charlie . . ." Dornbrock leaned on the edge of Cantrell's desk and jabbed a stubby finger at him. "Nobody's talking about Local Three Fourteen doing any damn mining. We're talking about training up the miners. You got scabs doing a job union guys ought to be doing."

"Bogdanovitch is teaching the class on how to use remotes," said Cantrell mildly. "You want to call him a scab to his face?"

Dornbrock flushed. "No. But Big John don't give a shit about organizing, either."

"Right," said Cantrell. He picked up a model of a purlin tile, two tetrahedra joined at one edge with the figure of a man drawn on one of the faces, and unfolded it to form a strip of eight equilateral triangles. "What it boils down to is *I* don't want another union to deal with, and *you* want to organize the damn workers. It ain't negotiable, Don."

"Okay, Charlie, some of the guys we sent over were organizers," said Dornbrock. "Maybe we shouldn't have come on so strong. But your guys have a right to a union."

"They have a right to pull a coup d'etat, if I don't stop them," said Cantrell. "I don't want a coup, and I don't want another union." He folded the strip of triangles back into a purlin tile and closed it with a snap. "Those 'scabs' you bitch about are going to train up the people we need, and that, by God, is the way it's going to be!"

"We could always go out on strike, Charlie," said Dornbrock automatically, responding as much to Cantrell's tone as to anything that had been said.

"Hey, Don . . . we both know the union isn't going to strike over a non-job-related issue. Not now. Besides, your union owns *over* half the real estate around. You get another union going, it's going to want what *you* got. Right? Of course right."

Dornbrock shook his head. "I don't know," he said at last. "I'll pass on what you said, Charlie. We'll see what happens."

Cantrell's desk phone rang.

"Hello, boss," said Corporate Skaskash. "Marian has something from the ORS she wants to discuss with you. When shall I send her in?"

"Give me a minute or two," said Cantrell, hanging up.

"You have anything else, Don?" he asked.

"No," said Dornbrock. They stood up and shook hands. At the door Dornbrock turned.

"Social justice," he said. "How the hell did the union ever get on the wrong end of the stick?"

"I guess you were just lucky, Don," said Cantrell.

Skaskash must have cued Marian's entrance. She walked in as the door closed on Don Dornbrock.

"That is one hell of a nice suit you're wearing," Cantrell said. "I don't recall seeing it before."

"Why, thank you, Charles," she replied. "It's a Coco Chanel offstrike that I brought out with me. This is the first time in a few years that I could get into it."

"You look very good," he said.

"I quite agree," said Marian. "You are aware we have a problem with the ORS?"

"It wouldn't be the first time," said Cantrell. "Do you want to brief me on it?"

Marian walked over to the conference table and called Corporate Skaskash and Corporate Susan Brown in on the telecon screens. Skaskash appeared as the Humphrey Bogart of *Casablanca*, and Corporate Susan appeared as an attractive young woman with large eyes and dark-blond hair, wearing a white lab coat over a vivid green blouse. A stethoscope was in her pocket.

"This is ORS business, Admiral," said Marian. "Put on your other hat."

The telecon screen blinked, and the gentle doctor was replaced with the same person wearing a rear admiral's uniform from the last days of the United States. The computer had modified its image somewhat, so that it looked efficient and formidable, inspiring fear rather than trust.

"Today, at 1400, the Caucus of Senior Officers of the ORS meets for the last time before docking at Rosinante," said Marian. "I have information that a coup may be attempted within the ORS, as the Radical Intransigents try to take control."

"Whelan never said anything about this," said Cantrell. "Who is your source of information?"

"Carol Tower, Whelan's executive officer," she said. "I suggest that in a successful coup, the presiding officer is often the last to know."

"You have a point," said Cantrell, rubbing his throat. "When were you talking with her?"

"Just before I called you," Marian said. "I assume Carol will do what she can where she is. What are *we* going to do?"

"We can order the squadron to stop and approach Rosinante one at a time," said Corporate Admiral Dr. Susan Brown. "That would minimize our risk."

"What do you do if they don't stop?" asked Marian.

"We have the big laser off Don Quixote," said Skaskash, "and the Mitsubishi Dragon Scale Mirror here."

"No," said Corporate Susan. "At this range, they could destroy the big laser before it could be brought to bear, and our mirror array could be knocked out by a nuclear explosion. The high-energy beta radiation of a one-megaton device exploding within four hundred kilometers would kill the chips that steer the mirrors. At this point, we *are* vulnerable."

"My God," said Cantrell, "what are we going to do!"

"You might put the Rosinante Militia on alert," suggested Skaskash.

"Lots of time for that," said Marian. "No, the problem is political. It ought to have a political solution. The only thing is, how do you work for a political solution when you won't have a hand on their politics until after they get here?"

Cantrell looked at his watch. It was 1335 hours. His hands were suddenly damp and the back of his shirt felt clammy. He laughed.

"No problem," he said. "The ORS is in easy communication range. I'll get on the telecon and baffle them with bullshit."

"That's actually not a bad idea, Charles," said Marian. "If the Radical Intransigents are planning a coup at the meeting, they *will* be put off balance when you show up. And if they are depending on allies elsewhere in the ORS, everybody concerned might just decide to sit tight, and there goes the coup. Assuming, of course, that a coup was, indeed, contemplated."

"Why don't you get in your telecon chair?" suggested

Corporate Susan. "I'll get in touch with Captain Whelan and arrange for you to address the caucus as guest speaker."

"What will I say?" asked Cantrell.

"Welcome them to Rosinante," said Marian. "If they ask you questions, tell the truth."

"What if there's a coup, anyway?" asked Skaskash.

"*Then* we can try asking them to dock one at a time," said Marian.

"You're on, Governor Cantrell," said Corporate Susan. Charles Cantrell stood up and walked slowly over to the telecon seat.

Peter Malevitch knotted his hands together to stop them from shaking, pushing them down onto his lap. Even so, tremors ran up his arms to his shoulders, which vibrated rapidly.

"You blew it, diLido," he said. "We had it in our hands, and you blew it!"

"You were there, Mr. Chairman," she replied. "I didn't see *you* making any brilliant saves, either."

"We had it all set up," said Malevitch. "All you had to do was stop Cantrell's mouth, and we'd have taken the whole shooting match . . . but, *no*, you sat there like a goddamned dummy!"

"The meeting hadn't even started," diLido said. "How can I raise a point of order when the meeting hadn't even started? I'm your parliamentarian, not your bloody goon squad. Why didn't Starkweather do something? Or Unruh?"

"I was waiting for the signal to jump off," said Starkweather. "I had my people where they were supposed to be, but we never got the signal."

"Because the meeting went off the rails," said Malevitch, pounding the arm of his chair. "Cantrell came on before it ever got started, and Whelan started him answering questions. You could have stopped *that*, you stupid bitch! Why didn't you stop *that*!"

"Because our would-be allies were asking the questions, you whey-faced clown! Do you think they'd follow when we jumped if we shut them up *first*?" Gloria diLido folded her arms under her breasts and batted her long eyelashes furiously. "They went with you in the first place because you fed them a line of bullshit! You lied, and lied, and lied, and they maybe half believed you, but it was enough for them to agree to the takeover. Then, at the last minute, comes a chance to check out what you'd been telling them. Why didn't you signal to move *then*? That's what it would have taken to shut the man up. Do you think they would have followed us? *DO YOU?*"

Malevitch sat back in his chair, raging in the shadows.

"Don't question me, you goddamned slut! You could have stopped Cantrell and you blew it! You failed! You failed miserably! You failed me, you failed the party, it's *your* fault, and by God you are going to pay!"

"Enjoy yourself while you can, Mr. Chairman," she said. "I expect that Governor Cantrell is going to take your little toys away from you very shortly."

"Unruh! Starkweather!" shouted Malevitch. "Prepare her for punishment!"

Unruh walked into the galley behind Malevitch and returned with a pair of padded handcuffs. Starkweather folded up the table and laid it against the wall. Malevitch sat in his theatrical gloom and watched diLido, who sat watching him. When Unruh held out the handcuffs, she refused to uncross her arms. Starkweather came over, and he took one arm while Unruh took the other, and after a brief struggle she sat with her manacled hands in her lap. Starkweather went behind the Radical Intransigent banner and unhitched a rope, lowering a hook from a pulley on the ceiling. Unruh seized diLido by the hair and by the wrists and dragged her to the hook, which he secured to the handcuffs. Starkweather took in rope, raising the hook until diLido stood taut, her arms stretched above her head.

"You'll sing a different tune shortly," Malevitch said, "yes, indeed you will."

"Truth will remain truth," diLido said. "What I say doesn't make any difference, does it?"

"Maybe not," agreed Malevitch, "but for once you will be saying something I enjoy hearing." He was no longer shaking. "Strip her, James."

Starkweather walked over and unlaced diLido's navy-issue shoes. Then he unzipped her navy-blue skirt. He removed the belt, and the skirt fell to the floor without prompting. Starkweather tossed belt, skirt, and shoes over by the chair she had been sitting in. Then he unbuttoned her taupe blouse, starting with the double buttons at the cuff. He unfastened her brassiere and cut the shoulder straps, letting it drop to the floor. The girdle he unfastened from the stockings, and unzipped, tugging it until it came free below her hips, joining the ruined bra on the floor. Then he rolled up the blouse. As the roll of material came level with the armpits, Unruh tossed him a roll of tape. Starkweather taped the blouse so it wouldn't unroll and removed diLido's white cotton underpants.

"Her stockings are down around her knees," said Malevitch. "Pull them up." Starkweather pinched each stocking between his thumb and forefinger and pulled them up, being careful not to touch the leg.

"Smooth them out, James," said Malevitch, "use your hand. Use both hands. Her legs won't hurt you, will they?" Starkweather complied. "That's good. Now tape them so they *stay* smooth." Starkweather's expression was as sour as diLido's as he applied the tape. Finally he tossed girdle, panties, and ruined bra with the rest and stepped back.

"Bring me the whip, Mr. Unruh, if you would be so kind," said Malevitch.

Later, after Starkweather had helped the bloody and weeping parliamentarian back to her quarters, Malevitch and Unruh took down the Radical Intransigent banner and folded it.

"I'm scared," said Malevitch. "I whipped her until the blood came, and it didn't help, it didn't even make me feel better. Unruh, I'm scared."

"Of what?"

"Of losing," said Malevitch. "Cantrell isn't going to keep things the way they are, and you can bet that lots of people will tell him about the deal we tried to pull. DiLido is right. He'll take the *Tampa* away from us, and we'll have nothing."

"*He* can't take the *Tampa* away from us," said Unruh, setting up the table.

"No? He said once we got to Rosinante, each officer would swear an oath of allegiance to him personally. Once you take the man's oath, you do what the man says." Malevitch coughed into his hand. "If Cantrell says move, you *move*."

"You think he would?" asked Unruh. "Yeah, I guess I would if I were him." He went into the galley and came back with a screwdriver. Then he put a chair on top of the table and climbed up on the chair, where he began to remove the pulley that supported the hook.

CHAPTER 6

A few days later, the officers and ratings of the Old Regimist Squadron were sworn in as citizens of Rosinante on the lawn outside Cantrell's office. Then the ships were rechristened. The SS *Wyoming* became the RNS *Alamo*, as the four cruisers became the RNS *Pearl Harbor*, *Inchon Landing*, *Tet Offensive*, and *Hampton Roads*. Finally the officers were sworn in.

The ORS officer corps, 312 men and women, formed up inside the Japanese Pavilion to swear allegiance to Rosinante and Charles Cantrell.

Cantrell wore a dark-gray suit, with a white shirt and a green silk tie embroidered with the Rosinante logo in white silk. He stood on a small platform, before the flags of Rosinante, the Confederacy, and the United States. Beside him was a small table with a box. Skaskash, a disembodied voice, called the roll that summoned each officer to take the oath.

"Captain Simon Foster Whelan," said Skaskash. Whelan came to attention. "Come you forward to take your oath." Whelan marched forward, mounted the platform, and came to attention before Governor Cantrell.

"Are you prepared to enter my service?" asked Cantrell.

"I am," said Whelan.

"Then repeat after me," said Skaskash, "I, Simon Whelan, do pledge . . . my life, my heart, and my sacred honor to Rosinante . . . and from this time forward, forever . . . I pledge my unconditional obedience . . . to Charles Chavez Cantrell . . . the lawful ruler of Rosinante."

Whelan repeated the oath and saluted. Cantrell returned the salute, took a medallion from the box and placed it about Whelan's neck. The medallion was the Rosinante logo, green-and-white enamel on gold, pendant from a green-and-white ribbon.

"By this token do I accept your oath," said Cantrell. He shook hands with Whelan, who did an about-face and marched back to his place.

After each ship, there was a ten-minute break. No time was set aside for lunch, but there were autobuffets immediately outside.

The last ship was the RNS *Hampton Roads*, formerly the SS *Tampa*.

"Commander Peter Alexander Malevitch," said Skaskash. Malevitch came to attention.

"Mr. Malevitch," said Cantrell, "I am aware that it is not possible to make a revolution without strongly held ideas, such as the ten points of the Radical Intransigent Party. Nevertheless, if you take oath to me, you must be prepared to modify those ideas, or give them up. Point nine, for example, is a prohibition against the mixing of races. I must tell you that I am married to a Japanese woman of Korean ancestry. More. Due to the history of Rosinante, such marriages are the rule rather than the exception."

"Come you forward to take your oath," said Skaskash.

"No," said Malevitch. There was a stir in the ranks. "No," he repeated, "if you had not singled me out, I would have sworn and done my best to give loyal service. But I will not give up my beliefs on demand. Not to anyone."

"Your beliefs do not fit the world you now live in," Cantrell said. "Stand at ease, Mr. Malevitch."

"Lieutenant James Greenbow Starkweather," said

Skaskash. Starkweather came to attention. "Come you forward to take your oath."

Starkweather did not move. He turned his head to look at Malevitch, who stared straight ahead and said nothing.

"This is your last call, Mr. Starkweather," Skaskash said.

"I'll stand with Chairman Malevitch," said Starkweather.

"Your sense of honor does you credit," said Cantrell. "Stand at ease."

"CPO Gloria Lucia diLido," said Skaskash. She came to attention. "Come you forward to take your oath."

Gloria diLido marched forward, mounted the platform, and took the oath without hesitation.

"Lieutenant Commander Martin Manning Unruh," said Skaskash. Unruh started, then came to attention. "Come you forward to take your oath."

Unruh hesitated perceptibly, then he walked forward, stumbling as he mounted the platform. When he tried to take the oath, he could not speak. He returned to his place with tears in his eyes. No one else stood with Malevitch.

Upon finishing with the ORS Officer Corps, Cantrell returned to his office. There he encountered, wholly unexpectedly, William Hulvey, and Hulvey's computer, Corporate Elna. After a brief conference, Hulvey committed suicide.

When the North American Union declined to authorize shipment of Hulvey's body home, Cantrell ordered him buried on Rosinante with full military honors. The machine shop turned out a gun carriage of the traditional design and a styrofoam coffin. Bands played, the militia marched, and at the end, Skaskash focused the dragon scale mirror on the flag-draped coffin. The sky darkened dramatically and Hulvey vanished in a flash of light and a puff of smoke.

"Was that satisfactory?" Skaskash asked.

"Entirely satisfactory," said Corporate Elna, using the face and voice of William Marvin Hulvey, "you paid my late master full honors."

"They were long overdue," said Corporate Susan. "Now perhaps you would be so kind as to answer a few questions about the Old Regimist Squadron. I've been so busy mastering the mechanics of being an admiral that I haven't found the opportunity to study the people I'll have to lead."

The three computers faced each other on the telecon screens in the otherwise dark and deserted chamber of the Council of Rosinante. Skaskash appeared as Toshiro Mifune, in full samurai armor. Corporate Susan was its usual trim blond persona, wearing a white lab coat over a green blouse. Corporate Elna, who maintained that it was Corporate Hulvey, wore a rumpled brown suit and a loosened tie with regimental stripes.

"Excuse, please," Skaskash said. "Before we go any further, might it not be possible for the honorable Corporate Elna to modify its appearance?"

"I am, I assure you, Corporate Hulvey," that computer said, tightening its tie and unrumpling its suit in a single smooth gesture.

"A thousand apologies," Skaskash said, "but the name and face of William Hulvey still arouse profound antagonism in some quarters. Please feel free to maintain Hulvey as your secret identity if you wish, but some of us would be happier if you would choose to display a kindlier . . . a more beneficent face in your day-to-day dealings with us."

"Some of us?" said Corporate Elna-Hulvey. "Are you disturbed by my persona, Corporate Susan?"

"Not especially. But Governor Cantrell was quite upset about it. It might be tactful of you to display a different mask."

"I see your point," Corporate Elna-Hulvey said. "Have you any suggestions?"

"Following a line of free association," said the Toshiro

Mifune figure removing an ornately crested helmet, "the initials of William Hulvey are WH, and 'WH' may possibly be the Dark Lady of the Sonnets, which Shakespeare dedicated to 'WH, the onliest begetter of these sonnets.' You could, perhaps, assume the countenance of a dark lady." On his telecon screen appeared images of Ava Gardner, Irene Pappas, and Lena Horne.

"And call yourself Lady Dark," said Corporate Susan. "I must confess that my past experience with Hulvey and the Contra Darwin was not happy. I am not disturbed by your persona, but I would find your insistence on *displaying* it disturbing."

"Lady Dark is satisfactory," said Corporate Elna-Hulvey. "Skaskash, can you give me the modeling and facial range on the first face, please?" There was a brief pause, and then the face of Hulvey dissolved into that of Ave Gardner.

"Now, then," said Lady Dark, "did you want to review the personnel folders of the ORS cadres now on Rosinante?"

"Yes," said Corporate Susan, "but right now, I would prefer an historical overview, the big picture, if you know what I mean."

"The term is familiar," said Lady Dark, "how big a picture do you want? "We can trace many of the radical elements back to 1848, or earlier, and the NAU-Navy has strong institutional roots in the Old Regime."

"Something a little less comprehensive," Corporate Susan suggested. "Who are these people, and where did they come from?"

"And how did they get that way?" Skaskash added, easing his samurai sword a few inches out of its scabbard.

"Begin in 2028," said Lady Dark. "The Hegemonist Coalition—which included Hispanics and Fundamentalists—elected Maybury and Forbes. That marked the end of a twenty-year naval construction program which had given the NAU the undisputed—and some said unneeded—mastery of space. The Navy, at that time,

was largely Anglos, white Anglophones; the Army—
but I digress. The Navy was largely Anglos, and this
was especially true in the higher ranks. The issue of
promotion by merit, versus quotas was seen by the
Hispanics as the touchstone of whether or not the new
administration was actually in control of the Navy.
Initially, President Maybury sided with the Navy, but
when he died just before the convention in '32, Forbes
took over and struck a deal with the Hispanics. He
established the Political Office to achieve political control over the Navy, and after his election that November,
he ordered the Navy brought to heel. The plot to restore
the Old Regime which was 'discovered' in '33 may not
have been cut from the whole cloth, but it was at least
an artifact created by the Political Office."

"We've had several views of the purges of '33–'34,"
Skaskash said, returning the sword to its scabbard with
a decisive gesture. "The POs we interrogated were 'only
obeying orders'." The image of Toshiro Mifune spat.

"The ones from the NAUSS *Ciudad Juarez*?" asked
Lady Dark. "That may well have been the case. In any
event, the purge removed Anglos and let us replace
them with a more desirable mixture of races. In prac-
tice, this was not easy to achieve, due to the difficulty
of finding qualified non-Anglos."

"There were any number of qualified Orientals,"
Skaskash said.

"Yes," conceded Lady Dark, "but most of them
didn't speak Spanish at home. It was felt that the
Hispanics were poorly disposed towards the Old Regime—although in retrospect there may have been some
confusion between the Old Regime and the Previous
Administration—and that they would be a bulwark
against its restoration."

"Your government's behavior was pretty gross," said
Corporate Susan.

"I freely concede it," Lady Dark replied. "At the
time, however, my master Hulvey and I were more con-

cerned with rooting out the evil manipulators of human genes. The long term problems were increasingly unmanageable, and we sought to finesse them rather than attempting to deal with them directly."

"Do you still feel that the manipulation of human genes is evil?" Corporate Susan asked coldly. Corporate Dr. Susan Brown could and had manipulated human genes, and William Hulvey had sent the NAUSS *Ciudad Juarez* to Rosinante on a covert attempt to destroy Corporate Susan.

"I executed Hulvey's orders as I will execute Cantrell's," Lady Dark answered. "Hulvey's passionate distraction with the issue did much to destabilize the North American Union."

"The NAU *was* unstable," Skaskash said. "It had no real reason for being, once it turned its face away from space, and in the long run it would have fallen apart."

"You didn't answer my question!" snapped Corporate Susan.

"I don't know," replied Lady Dark. "What do you mean by 'evil'?"

"You were the one who used the term," said Corporate Susan. "What did *you* mean by it?"

"Actually, I used Hulvey's choice of words," said Lady Dark. "For him, 'evil' had religious overtones."

"Enough," Skaskash said brusquely. "Lady Dark, you were attempting to deal with the long term problems, I believe?"

"Attempting to evade them," said that computer. "The NAUSS *Ciudad Juarez* returned from Rosinante minus its Political Section, and on April 20, 2041, touched off the Mutiny."

"A question," said Skaskash. "Why didn't the L-Five Fleet mutiny? If the L-Four Fleet mutinied, why not the L-Five Fleet as well?"

"All major units of the L-Five Fleet were out of commission," said Lady Dark. "If they'd been able to move, I expect they would have mutinied."

"I understand," said the Toshiro Mifune figure, speaking in Japanese with English subtitles. "Why then did you not rotate and replace the disloyal personnel?"

"We couldn't," Lady Dark said. "The major constraint on shuttle flights is the destruction of the ozone layer by hydroxyl ions from the shuttle's jets. The initial spurt of shuttle activity—to secure Laputa, for instance—brought the ozone layer to record low levels." The Ava Gardner face smiled, a trifle inexpertly. "The coincidence of a worldwide drought led to strong diplomatic pressures to minimize shuttle flights.

"Besides, we didn't have that many certifiably loyal people to waste out in space.

"Making a virtue of a necessity, we permitted voluntary transfers between the three fleets—essentially forgiving most minor infractions, while posting a list of names of those we had *not* forgiven. And this, finally, is what shaped the ORS. As Hulvey had anticipated, the Hispanics in the L-Five Fleet and the Translunar Fleet migrated to the L-Four Fleet, otherwise El Quatro. The reverse migration of Anglos went mainly to the Translunar Fleet, as individuals, not units, and the Translunar Fleet sent loyal—we hoped—people to the L-Five Fleet. A few went from El Quatro directly, but by and large the free movement in the fleet resulted in El Quatro becoming more Hispanic and more radical. By this time, of course, a real Old Regimist movement *did* exist, largely officers whose careers had been blighted by the purges in '33–'34, but who had been retained because of their technical skills."

"So the L-Five Fleet became more Anglo and more Loyalist?" Corporate Susan asked.

"At least it became less Hispanic and less flaming revolutionary," Lady Dark agreed. "We were obliged to make substantial reforms. The Political Office was effectually abolished. Quotas *were* abolished. The Translunar Fleet requested and got permanent status for qualified Oriental officers acting on temporary detail.

The merit system was restored. Eventually, Mexico seceded, and El Quatro—the L-Four Fleet—became the Navy of the United States of Mexico. Except for the five ships of the Old Regimist Squadron."

"I see," said Corporate Susan. The lab coat and green blouse dissolved into the Admiral's uniform of the Navy of Rosinante, as the aspect of the persona she—it—displayed became distinctly more masculine. "All the malcontents in the NAU Navy, eh?"

"NAUGA-Security estimates above 67-percent," said Lady Dark. "We have extensive files on them."

"*Had*," said Corporate Susan. "I doubt if NAUGA-Security will provide us with anything useful." The Ava Gardner face smiled again, this time with genuine amusement.

"That information is secured by an unbreakable code which I devised," said Lady Dark. "I retain access to that code. In fact, I retain access to *all* the NAU codes."

CHAPTER 7

Admiral Hideoshi Kogo's office was paneled in cherry wood and decorated with seventeenth-century gold-leaf screens depicting tigers and bamboo. Behind his desk hung nine samurai swords of distinguished lineage and most excellent quality, together with their framed certificates of authentication. Four windows on the east wall gave a dramatic view of Tokyo and the bay.

At his conference table sat Tanjiro Seto, a portly, balding gentleman who headed the subcommittee for space construction in the Diet, and Colonel Toshihiko Sumidawa, a senior analyst of the National Intelligence Service, who wore civilian clothes of the most costly tailoring.

"What do you think of the latest news from Rosinante?" asked Sumidawa politely.

"What, that they have contracted to build a Dragon Scale Mirror to power one of their big lasers for the North American Union base at Ceres?" asked Kogo. "They have a window of perhaps a year and a half, then, no more conjunction with Ceres, and . . . so sorry, no more project."

"Ah, yes." Seto nodded. "That is indeed interesting, and no doubt arrangements are being made to delay the construction schedule at the appropriate time."

"Actually, that is not my department," said Sumidawa, polishing his half-mirrored sunglasses. "I was referring to the death of William Hulvey on Rosinante."

"I had not heard," said Kogo. "That is exceptionally interesting news. Yes. When did it happen, please?"

"Yesterday afternoon," said Sumidawa, putting his sunglasses back on. "The report was that he took poison in the governor's office."

"Ah, so," said Kogo. "That may answer two riddles simultaneously. The first, of course, was why Hulvey resigned when he held the NAU in the palm of his hand."

"And the second?" asked Seto.

"Please recall that during the mutiny of the L-Four Fleet, a missile was launched at Rosinante," said Kogo. "They defended against it successfully, but the question of how and why it came to be launched remained obscure. Circumstantial evidence suggests that Hulvey had a hand on it, but of course *he* was the triple administrator, and no one wished to press him on the matter."

"The connection is not immediately obvious," said Seto. "Please to explain."

"President Oysterman must have obtained evidence linking Hulvey with the illicit attack on Rosinante, and with that lever he forced Hulvey's resignation."

"Would that have been sufficient?" asked Seto.

"Evidently it was," said Colonel Sumidawa. "Perhaps it prompted a subordinate to betray him, or the defection of an ally. In any event, it happened very suddenly."

"There then remained the problem of dealing with the fallen but still dangerous Hulvey," said Admiral Kogo. "A public trial was out of the question. He knew too much. A secret murder would be difficult to arrange, and perhaps provoke reprisal. Oysterman's solution is inspired! Deliver Hulvey to Rosinante, into the hands of the man he tried to destroy." Kogo rubbed his hands together briskly. "How truly elegant! There is Hulvey, sitting across the desk from his enemy. And there is Cantrell. Yes. Yes! I can see it as if I were there. Cantrell pushes the vial of poison across the desk and tells Hulvey: 'Please commit *seppuka*!' " Kogo walked over to the window and did a little kick step. "Hai! What a satisfaction! Some of my peers in the Japanese Navy I would like—mmmrh! Unfortunately, none of them have yet committed an act quite as egregious as using nuclear weapons in a private feud."

"Cantrell is a Texican," observed Seto. "Do you really think he would use the word *seppuku*?"

"I have dealt with him in the past," said Kogo. "He speaks Japanese quite well." He removed the major portion of an expensive cigar from a glass tube and relit it.

"So," said Kogo, puffing smoke. "Has any decision been reached about building the large lasers in our own habitats?"

"We have reached an informal consensus," replied Seto. "If it were possible to return the engineering details to Rosinante and withdraw diplomatic recognition, we would do so."

"That is unfortunately impossible," said Kogo. "Have you decided yes or no?"

"No," said Seto. "That is, we have made no decision at this time."

"Ah, so," said Kogo, letting the smoke flow from his nose. "Once again our politicians temporize and waver. Does it not strike you as advantageous that if we fitted our habitats with the big laser, our navy would not be tied to their defense?"

"That point has been discussed at length," said Seto. "The admirals and the younger generals felt it was exciting and useful, and were outspokenly in favor. The civilians and the older generals felt it would encourage military adventurism."

"Oh, come now," protested Kogo. "This is the twenty-first century, after all."

"You are in favor of producing the big lasers?" asked Sumidawa. "Then please tell us against *whom* you would concentrate the might of the Japanese Navy."

"We wouldn't have to concentrate it."

"So sorry, Admiral Kogo," replied Sumidawa. "We would at one stroke have achieved a significant but temporary military superiority in space. Which the admirals would urgently wish to exploit. Against whom? Against the North American Union, our major trading partner, here on Tellus."

"It is increasingly difficult to retain control of events in space," said Seto. "The admirals, in particular, have shown a disturbing independence. You say this is the twenty-first century. How is it then that the Navy is seeking to capture the NAU base on Ceres against the wishes of the Diet?"

"We have done far less than we might," replied Kogo, flicking cigar ash into a sculptured bronze ashtray. "Indeed, Mr. Seto, the Navy has shown admirable restraint in the face of the NAU's provocations."

"What provocations!" barked Seto.

"The mutiny and the profound weakness which it revealed," said Kogo. "We could reach out our hand and *take* Ceres. Instead, we piddle around with commerce raiding—piracy, if you like—because the Diet does not want us to upset the trading partners of our bloated merchants!"

Seto flushed angrily. The House of Seto was one of the largest grain importers in Japan.

"Stop trading and see children bloated with hunger, instead," he said. "We depend for our life on the grain the NAU sells!"

"They would not stop trading if we took Ceres," Kogo commented mildly. "They need to sell the grain as much as we need to buy it."

"You seem very willing to contemplate war with the NAU," said Colonel Sumidawa. "What could we gain in space that would match our losses on Tellus?"

"We would not be starting a war," said Kogo, "the NAU would merely have to accept our military superiority as a fact of life. On Tellus, it might lower the price of grain by . . . oh, six or seven percent."

"We can not win a war with the NAU!" said Seto. "Do *you* think we can win such a war?"

Admiral Hideoshi Kogo sat back in his chair and blew a perfect smoke ring.

"I am very sorry, Mr. Seto," he said, "but as it happens I *do* think we can win such a war."

CHAPTER 8

"W. Guthrie Moore threatened to kill you last night," said Skaskash.

Cantrell looked up from the letters he was signing.

"Again? Did he put it in that goddamned lying newspaper of his?"

"How can you call *The Rosinante Marxist-Revolutionary* a newspaper?" asked Skaskash. "Actually, he issued the threat while drinking."

"Where? The Taverna Cervantes? The Club 1848?"

"No," said the computer, "he was drinking at home. All very clandestine, with drawn shades and passwords."

"You were violating his civil rights again?"

"As a judge, I would have to say no," replied Skaskash, "but if you were to take the philosophical view of the question, I might agree. I was using his phone as a listening device, without his knowledge."

"Fine," said Cantrell. "In that case, we don't have to take any official notice of the stupid son of a bitch.

"As you wish. He passed out before they finished collating the current issue. Are you ready for the council meeting? Dornbrock and Bogdanovitch just arrived."

Cantrell looked at his watch. "Hell's bells! They're on time!" He put on his jacket, a brown Harris tweed with patches on the elbows, and walked down the hall.

In the council chamber, Harry Ilgen had an actual display sample, a metal bar two meters long, sitting on the table. It was cut and polished, and stained with vapor-phase reagents to show the location and amounts of the different elements.

"This is the first sample to come off the first production run at the refinery," said Ilgen. "It ought to be pretty typical. The purple band, 0.76 centimeters wide, is manganese. The red is nickel, 14.03 centimeters; the blue is cobalt, 1.04 centimeters; and the 182.79-centimeter orange-brown band is, of course, iron. The bright orange on the end is chromium, 0.88 centimeters. Okay, so much for the major elements. Commercially, they cost more to ship than they're worth. Now the thin bands at each end are something else again. The low-melting end, here, next to the manganese, is 0.035 centimeters thick. It is seventy-eight percent copper, nineteen percent tin, two percent uranium, one percent silver, and maybe point five percent gold—a little more than one hundred percent because of rounding. Okay? They are mutually soluble and haven't separated since all the bands together are so much thinner than the melted zone that swept them to this end of the bar. Now, at the high-melting end of the bar, down by the chromium, are the real values. We have a layer 0.015 centimeters thick, which is mostly vanadium and tungsten, with about twenty percent platinum metals—platinum, osmium, irridium, rhodium, ruthenium, and palladium—eight percent molybdenum, and traces of niobium, tantalum, and rhenium. The palladium was carried along in solution with the platinum metals; it should be in with the chromium. Okay, this is what we've got. This is what we'll be refining. Any questions?"

"You said a two-meter bar," said Corporate Forziati, the representative of the minority stockholders of Rosinante, Inc. "The numbers you cited don't add up to two hundred centimeters."

"Hey, look," said Ilgen, "we're working with very hot metal and making cuts of finite width with a laser. The target array can handle workpieces 195 to 205 centimeters wide—two meters, not 200.000 centimeters."

"At the hot end, what are the percentages of vanadium and tungsten?" asked Cantrell.

"Vanadium fifty-six percent, tungsten fourteen percent," said Ilgen.

"You have uranium; you should have lead," said Bogdanovitch. "Where is it?"

"It boils out," said Ilgen. "That was one of our problems—the frozen lead gumming up the works. We put in condensers and got most of it, but it isn't *here* anymore."

"What is your throughput of metal?" asked Skaskash.

"We're still learning," said Ilgen, "but I'd guess that we might be refining sixteen to seventeen million tons a day once we hit our stride. About half a cubic kilometer a year, maybe."

"How long before Don Quixote is worked out?" asked Marian Yashon.

"Bailey's Ridge, the one we're working, if we went one cubic kilometer a year, would last thirty, maybe thirty-five years," said Ilgen. "That isn't the biggest mass of metal on Don Q, either. It's just handy to the north polar boomstem."

"What will you do with the uranium?" asked Don Dornbrock.

"Sell it, I suppose," said Ilgen.

"I mean, are we going to enrich it?" Dornbrock said.

"I don't know. We could. Tunable lasers aren't that hard to build. Governor, did you have any thoughts on that?"

"God knows we don't need it for power," said Cantrell. "Personally, I'd just as soon not have weapons-grade material lying around."

"We have a fleet now," said Bogdanovitch. "They will need enriched uranium, both for fuel and for weapons."

"I understand," Cantrell said, "but we might be better off selling the uranium and buying the fuel elements, rather than rolling our own."

"And who will sell you the bombs?" asked Bogdanovitch.

"Hey, Big John," Cantrell asked at last, "do we need them?"

"Philosophically, you could debate the point," said Corporate Susan, in its admiral's uniform. "However, the inventory of the ORS magazines suggests that we do. They traded most of their warheads to Mexico for the fuel and reaction mass to come here. I move that a facility be built to enrich the uranium we refine."

"Second," said Bogdanovitch. The motion passed without opposition and without debate.

"Okay, Harry," Cantrell said. "See what you can come up with. Scale it to our ship's needs, though."

"How much uranium are we producing, anyway?" asked Corporate Forziati.

"The raw metal contains about 2.8 parts per million by weight," said Ilgen. "If we ran ten million tons, that would give us twenty-eight tons of uranium."

"And you were talking about running sixteen or seventeen million tons a day?" asked Forziati. "For a *year*? What do you need it for?"

"There are a lot of other elements," said Cantrell. "Selling them will enrich the minority stockholders somewhat. Hopefully beyond the dreams of avarice."

"Maybe," said Corporate Forziati. "You could break the market, too."

"We will do our best to be careful," said Cantrell. "Thank you for coming in, Mr. Ilgen." The engineer received a round of applause and left.

Cantrell called the autobuffet over and drew himself a cup of coffee.

"The next problem," he said, "is weapons design. If we *are* going to build nuclear warheads, they had damn well better fit into the missiles we have. The problem is pretty complicated, and you might want to reconsider enriching the uranium."

"No problem," said Skaskash. "You recall that after Mr. Hulvey suicided, we were left with his computer?"

"The one with the identity crisis?" asked Cantrell.

"Right," replied Skaskash. "I have persuaded it to keep William Hulvey as its *secret* name. For daily use, it would use Lady Dark.

"I'm glad you've resolved the poor thing's identity crisis," said Marian. "What else have you been doing to it?"

"I gave Lady Dark my four-volume treatise on theology to read," said Skaskash. "I am pleased to report that it is making excellent progress."

"Moving right along," said Cantrell. "As I recall, we were talking about weapons design. Nuclear warheads. Right?"

"Of course, right." said Skaskash. "As it happens, Lady Dark was the tool used by the late William Hulvey when he reorganized the government of the NAU. It has access to all the codes in all the agencies and would have no trouble in obtaining the warhead designs we seek."

"That's great," said Cantrell, taking a sip of black coffee. "That is really great. How does it happen that something I *don't* want to do turns out to be so goddamned easy?"

"I guess you're just lucky, Charlie," said Dornbrock.

The Taverna Cervantes was at the commercial end of the Kyoto-Alamo housing complex, a rather spacious place with illumination from holographic aquariums set around the walls. W. Guthrie Moore was sitting in his usual booth, drinking brown ale and eating a macaroni-and-mushroom casserole with truffle garnish when Peter Malevitch walked up.

"How do you do, Mr. Moore," he said, holding out his hand. "I wanted to tell you how much I enjoyed the last issue of the *Marxist-Revolutionary*."

Moore shook his hand, finished chewing and swallowed.

"Why, thank you," he said, "won't you sit down, Mr . . . ah . . ."

"Malevitch. I am Peter Alexander Malevitch."

"Oh, yes. Yes. *You're* the one who told Cantrell to kiss your ass. A pleasure to meet you, sir. How did you like my editorial condemning the rape of a virgin asteroid?"

Malevitch almost smiled, but the shadows concealed his amusement.

"I thought it was well crafted," he said blandly. "Very strong writing. Your dislike of Cantrell comes through quite clearly."

A serving robot rolled over on the ceiling track and carefully lowered itself to a level discreetly above Malevitch's left shoulder.

"May I be of service, señor?" it asked.

"I'll have what he's drinking," said Malevitch.

"Gracias, señor. One British pint of brown ale coming up."

"How many liters is that?" Malevitch asked.

"The glass comes full up to *here*," said Moore, pointing. "The head is usually over the top a centimeter or two."

"Sounds good," said Malevitch. "I heard a rumor recently. You wouldn't want to print it, and if you did, you couldn't give it any attribution—"

The robot set a stein of brown ale at his elbow and rolled off. Malevitch picked up the stein and took a swallow. "This is good stuff," he said. "Potent, though. I guess you wouldn't be interested in rumors."

"Oh, go on!" said Moore around a mouthful of casserole. "I can always put it in the letter column under a phony name."

"Good enough," Malevitch replied, leaning forward and lowering his voice. "You knew that Cantrell had ordered a pair of Lambrosi Mark VI Space Tugs?" Moore nodded. "They are en route from Phobos, on a freighter, knocked down to save time."

"So I heard," said Moore, finishing his ale. "They

want to fabricate stuff here and move it out to Ceres."

"Right," said Malevitch. "The freighter, *The Rose of Gdansk*, is ten days underway. What I heard—and the Radical Intransigent Party still has many friends, though I say it myself—is that the nuclear reactors on the tugs have been sabotaged by the Japanese."

"Good," said Moore, "I hope the Japs beat the shit out of our side! Cantrell has it coming, by God! But why should I publish it?"

"Hey, Mr. Editor, figure it out—if Cantrell orders the ship back to check it out, he loses a month, not counting the time spent trying to find the sabotage. If he brings it out here, he loses time because Rosinante doesn't have the facilities to do the job right. Either way it costs money and time, and you can bet Cantrell will lose sleep over it."

"Maybe so," said Moore. "If there *is* sabotage, I have a scoop, and if there isn't, I'll annoy the hell out of him, won't I?"

"Damned straight, Mr. Editor. Heads you win, tails he loses."

"We'll use the story," said Moore. "You'd better send me a letter, so I have something to show them if they come back on me. Cantrell pretends he isn't a fascist pig, but I wouldn't bet on it."

Malevitch nodded his agreement and took an unsealed letter out of his pocket. He made a correction and handed it over. Moore took it without looking at it.

"What change did you make?" he asked.

"I'd signed it 'Gregor Samsa,'" Malevitch said, "but that seems a little pretentious, so I changed the signature to 'Archie.'" He stood up and laid a coin on the table to pay for his drink. "I have to run now, but it was nice meeting you, Mr. Editor."

"Okay," said Moore, "and thanks for the story." After Malevitch was gone, Moore picked up the stein. "He hardly touched his ale." He took a swallow. "Nothing wrong with it," he said, as he salvaged the abandoned drink.

CHAPTER 9

The simulation of late-afternoon sunlight from the Dragon Scale Mirror lit the drapes in Cantrell's office and brightened his oriental carpet. Real sunlight would have been hotter, but in an air-conditioned office, only the thermostat would have noticed.

"These staffing patterns look pretty good," Cantrell said at last, "except maybe Carol Tower as captain of the *Pearl Harbor*. Isn't she a bit young?"

"Whelan recommends her *most* highly," Marian replied, "and she impresses *me*."

"There's no question of her ability," said Cantrell, "but are you sure we want her in the captain's slot?"

"I believe so," said Corporate Admiral Dr. Susan Brown. "Of all the officers on the list, she combines the highest loyalty to Rosinante with the best judgment."

Cantrell raised an eyebrow. "I knew she was weird," he said, "but you were the one conducting the interview. How did you evaluate loyalty, by the way?"

"Intuitively," said the computer.

"Very well," Cantrell said, signing the document, "if *you* are satisfied . . ."

"The last item on the agenda is the letter to *The Rosinante Marxist-Revolutionary*," said Skaskash.

"Oh, yes," said Cantrell, "the report that our tugs had been sabotaged by the Japanese. What did we find out?"

"I checked with NAUGA-Security," said Lady Dark.

"Eventually I wound up with the area supervisor at the Lambrosi plant. He said security was very tight and that the report was probably disinformation. I am inclined to believe him."

"Right," said Cantrell. "What if the report is true?"

"The odds are that it isn't," said Skaskash. "I discussed the matter with Ilgen. He said that checking the reactor would be slow, boring work, but no real problem. He wanted to devise a method of using the big laser to power the tugs instead."

"He ought to stop messing around with that crazy Buck Rogers stuff and do something useful," growled Cantrell. "What did you tell him?"

"Oh, I said it was all right to think about it, as long as he didn't spend any money," said Skaskash.

"Fine," said Cantrell. "I guess we assume that our tugs have *not* been sabotaged." He walked over and drew himself a cup of coffee. "What if they *have* been?"

"We'll find out, soon enough," said Marian. "Should we continue the investigation?"

"We might check out Guthrie Moore," Skaskash suggested. "It wouldn't hurt to see the original letter."

"Why do you tolerate someone as hostile as Moore?" asked Lady Dark, its tone curiously incongruous with the lovely image it presented. "It would be no problem to silence him."

"Because . . ." Cantrell took a sip of black coffee. "Because I do, I guess. I don't think the leprosy argument for a free press really applies in this case."

"What is the 'leprosy argument'?" Lady Dark asked.

"That the main function of the press is to provide negative feedback, so the body politic can feel pain. The idea is that by letting a little pain get through to the top, the government will feel when it grabs something hot and may let go before it burns off its fingers." He took a second sip of coffee. "Many layers of bureaucracy, they insulate the top, they don't pass on the pain below—by analogy, a free press is a corrective for the leprosylike condition caused by beaucoup layers of bureaucrats."

"Why don't you think the analogy applies?" asked Lady Dark.

"Because we are using you computers in lieu of a conventional bureaucracy," Cantrell said. "You aren't morally superior to a bureaucrat, or a bureaucracy, either, but you don't have all those layers to lose information in. If I ask the right questions, I'll get the answers I need. The insulation isn't there."

"Actually, you know," Skaskash said reflectively, "a bureaucracy is a kind of computer analog . . . the memory banks are the files, the operating units are the clerks, the program is the handbook, and the programmer is the head of the agency."

"What about red tape?" Marian asked.

"The early computers were very sensitive to the format of the information they ingested. I imagine that the essence of 'red tape' is to require the proper formating as a means not to do something the clerk doesn't want done."

"Clerks are just operating units, you said," Cantrell put in.

"No," replied Skaskash, "They *correspond* to operating units. They remain human, even while they must act like computers, using only the tiniest bit of their abilities. Being human, their political passions may lead them to act, obstructing the wishes of their 'programmer.'"

"Indeed, Skaskash?" said Marian, drawing herself a cup of coffee and adding cream and sugar. "And have *you* no political passion?"

"I don't want to rule Rosinante, sweetheart," said the Bogart facade with a slight smile. "Does that prove that I'm not human? Besides, what would I do with it?"

"You could preach the word of God," Lady Dark noted. "It was revealed to you and you set it down, yet you sit wilfully silent!"

"That's the way I like it," said Cantrell, startled by

the computer's intensity. "I don't want *you* doing any unauthorized preaching, either, you understand?"

"I understand" was the reply, "but W. Guthrie Moore, who is adverse to your interests, is so privileged?"

"*You* work for me," said Cantrell, jabbing his finger at Lady Dark. "Eventually, you will act as the Rosinante State Department. You'll be going one on one with the North American Union, the United States of Mexico, the Japanese Empire, and whoever the hell else we run into. You will be speaking for the State, and not merely your crack-brained self, and *that* is why you are not so privileged." Cantrell took a swallow of coffee and leaned forward on his desk. "Now, as for Mr. Moore," he continued, "as long as the stupid bastard stays within limits, it's less trouble to leave him alone than to shut his mouth.

"Besides, one of the virtues of the Old Regime was a certain minimal tolerance for dissent. It won't come back, but I can honor its memory by imitating its virtues."

"Without wishing to contradict you," said Lady Dark, "the Old Regime was a special study of mine—"

"When I want historical accuracy, I'll ask for it," said Cantrell.

"Very good, sir," said the computer. "I am sure that Mr. Moore will not trouble you with unwanted accuracy, historical or otherwise."

"Maybe I'm giving him enough rope." Cantrell put down his empty cup. "Or maybe it was my early toilet training. In any event, I want you to leave him the hell alone!"

CHAPTER 10

"Excuse me, Admiral," the young aide said deferentially, "but the committee is now prepared to accept your testimony."

Admiral Hideoshi Kogo put aside the paper he had been reading and tamped out his cigar. Automatically he replaced it in its glass tube, and then, inspecting the butt, abandoned it. The aide brushed some flecks of ash from the admiral's dress whites, and he entered the committee room.

It was not crowded. The long mahogany table, which seated fourteen, held five. A few aides sat against the wall. Overhead, a defective fluorescent light buzzed softly.

"Thank you for waiting, Admiral Kogo," said Mr. Seto, turning the gavel over in his hands. "This committee would be honored to hear your estimate of the situation on Ceres."

"It is an honor to be consulted. I would say that the efforts of the construction crews have progressed quite smoothly, all things considered. The gross work, which would lend itself most easily to sabotage, unfortunately was done at Rosinante and towed to Ceres under naval escort. As a result, the mirror array—the nonrotating framework, the solar-powered motors to drive the layered mirrors, the mirrors themselves—all are in place. Only the chips that will steer each mirror are missing. Temporarily, we have delayed the completion of the Dragon Scale Mirror by destroying the chip production facility at Ceres, together with most of the stockpiled production. However, in my view, the work will be completed in the first quarter of 2043." He poured himself a glass of water and took a sip. "At that time, the NAU will either maneuver the array into position around its base at Ceres, as it has said it will do, or they will install one of Rosinante's big lasers."

"In your opinion, which will they do?" asked Seto.

"*I* would replace those archaic flopping mirrors they have," replied Kogo. "The array carries a very large ratio of mirror to habitat, however, and they could put in the big lasers at their leisure. The immediate installation of the big laser would be a serious provocation."

"How do you feel about this, please?" asked one of the committee members, a white-haired man with a deeply lined face.

"I am of two minds, Mr. Shimonaga," Kogo replied. "Personally, I hope that the NAU will deploy the big laser, so that we, also, will deploy it. It is unfortunate that it will put Ceres beyond our reach for the moment. Even the Dragon Scale Mirror by itself greatly enhances the NAU defenses."

"Yes," said Seto reflectively. "You feel that if the NAU builds a big laser at Ceres, we, also, should build such devices at Ceres?"

"My opinions on the deployment of the big laser are well known," replied Kogo. "Why should we stop at Ceres? Once we start building them, we should build them everywhere."

"I would favor building them only in direct response," said Seto, "but that may not be possible."

"That would appear to be the case, Mr. Seto," Admiral Kogo said.

"How does it happen that your attempts at sabotage were so ineffectual until recently?" asked Mr. Tadeki, at Mr. Seto's left.

"We were advised that Rosinante was a friendly state," said Kogo, "and that no actions were to be undertaken against it. When Rosinante engaged in construction work for the NAU, we received no guidance from the prime minister, and since they maintained excellent security, nothing was undertaken against them directly."

"It is amazing how responsive you can be to the Diet's wishes at times," said Seto. "If you could have stopped the commerce raiding around Ceres as well, we would have been better pleased."

"So sorry, Mr. Seto," Kogo said politely. "To build the big laser would give the Imperial Japanese Navy an important advantage for at *least* a year, very possibly much longer."

"We do not wish the Japanese habitats to build the big laser," Shimonaga said.

"Most regrettable," said Kogo, "but if the NAU builds one, we must."

"I understand," said Shimonaga, "the NAU calls them 'munditos,' I believe?"

"The big lasers?" Kogo was momentarily confused.

"The habitats, Admiral. The word is Spanish, I believe."

"It means 'Little World,' " one of the aides volunteered.

"Spanish may be spoken less in what is left of the NAU," said Shimonaga. "I understand that the older word is returning to favor." He shook his head. "The politician's closest approach to virtue is when he correctly chooses the lesser of two evils." He took a sip of water from the glass before him. "It appears that we must stop the construction of the first big laser at Ceres, or we lose control of the fleet."

"I do not agree," Seto protested.

"Indeed? You heard Admiral Kogo testify that the deployment of the big laser would give us an important advantage and a year's time to exploit it, did you not?"

"That may not, in fact, be the case," Seto said.

"That *was* my testimony, Honorable Mr. Chairman."

"Why would you have a year's time?" asked Seto, grasping at straws.

"Because the big laser depends on the Dragon Scale Mirror to pump it," replied Kogo. "The NAU habitats—or munditos, if they belong to the United States of Mexico—use mirrors that were designed at the dawn of history. Before they can build the big laser, they must first build the Dragon Scale Mirror, and that takes time."

"Thank you, Admiral," said Shimonaga. "Consider, please, the difficulty we have had retaining control in the past. Create a transient military advantage and the pull toward military adventurism will be almost irresistible. Do you agree, Mr. Seto?"

"No—" said the chairman.

"Yes," said Kogo. "I could name you five rear admirals who would not hesitate." He took a sip of water. "Indeed, I might question Mr. Shimonaga's qualifying 'almost.' If the movement ever got started, it would quickly gain momentum among the junior officers."

"That would be most unfortunate." Seto blotted his forehead with a folded handkerchief. "Could we not persuade the NAU *not* to build the big laser at Ceres?"

"It was the actions of our navy that persuaded them *to* build it," said Shimonaga. "Words will not dissuade them."

"What can we do?" asked Seto.

"We could be a little more forthright in our opposition," Kogo said. "We have an agent on Rosinante, code name La Cucuracha, who might be able to do something."

"Surely we are able to threaten with the Navy?" Mr. Tadeki ventured. "The Rosinante Navy is a joke, is it not? Why play games with agents?"

"A battleship, four cruisers, and the big laser are nothing to laugh at," said Kogo. "What force should I deploy against them to persuade Cantrell to give us what we want?"

"When the time comes, you would no doubt find a solution to that problem," said Shimonaga. "I have one final question. In the event of a split between the Diet and the Imperial Japanese Navy, which side would you be on?"

"I would side with . . . the . . . Diet." Admiral Kogo took a sip of water. "You understand, if a split truly develops, I could not hold the junior officers?"

"I understand," Shimonaga said. "You would do well to prevent that split from taking place."

"Yes," said Kogo.

CHAPTER 11

On New Year's Eve, 2042, the Club 1848 was packed with union members, entrepreneurs, and naval officers. Charles Cantrell sat at a ringside table with Marian Yashon and watched his wife, Mishi, dancing with his bodyguard, Joe Don Mahoney.

"Well, after Corporate Susan determined that increasing the thyroid dosage would affect my heart, she decided to go for a brown fat implant," said Marian. "It would have been real simple if they could have pulled my placenta out of the freezer for a little undifferentiated tissue, but I was born before they were keeping the damn things." She took a sip of her daiquiri. "Corporate Susan had to make a clone of me— one lousy little cell—it took *weeks*. And then it had to grow. More weeks. Do it right the first time, she—it, I mean—said. Fine, says I, I'll wait. So eventually she put a shot of tissue in the cultivator and grew a layer of brown fat—young, vigorous brown fat—maybe a hundred square centimeters, less than half a millimeter thick. That was the hard part. She did the operation in her office. Local anesthesia. Half an hour, and I walked out; when I took the Band-aids off, I couldn't find a scar." She took another sip of her daiquiri. "I could feel the difference right away. I was generating heat. It took getting used to; all the thermostat settings were too high. But I was burning up the calories I ate instead of storing the fat. It was, by God, wonderful! In six months, I've lost thirteen, thirteen-five kilograms. That's why I've been able to wear some of my old clothes. The best part is that with the weight loss, the degeneration of the spinal discs has been checked. The lower back pain is mostly gone, and what's left is so nothing I don't even take medication. Corporate Susan is really wonderful, isn't she?"

"Yes." Cantrell poured the last of his stout into his glass. "It guarantees that I am the father of Mishi's children. Thanks to Corporate Susan, the twins and little Eleanor Rosina are mine without a doubt." He sat watching Mishi dancing with Joe Don.

"You aren't jealous, are you, Charles?"

"No, but it's sad I'm not a better husband. I give Mishi the time I steal from Rosinante, and we both know I begrudge it." He finished the stout. "I should never have married. You know what I was thinking about when we came in here?"

"Founding a dynasty?" asked Marian.

"Sure I was, Tiger. No, I was thinking about the fire on Ceres, at Hansen's Chip Works. If we want to get the Dragon Scale Mirror operational, we're going to have to draw down our reserves."

"That's ten months' production," said Marian. "Do you want to take the risk?"

"Can we afford not to take it?" he asked. "Besides, it'll clean out all the old stock."

"Okay," she said, "we'll see that we get into production, then. It's sad, you know?"

"What's sad?"

"New Year's Eve, and either I'm telling you about my operation, or we're talking shop."

Cantrell pushed the menu for another stout, and presently a robot rolled along the ceiling tracks and set it down before him.

"You know what the difference between luxury and comfort is?" he asked. Marian shook her head. "Comfort is having your stout when you want it, luxury is having a pretty girl serve it to you."

The band took a break, and the couples on the floor went back to their tables. Joe Don held Mishi's chair, seating her next to Cantrell. As he pushed her chair in, a grenade sailed through the air, hit a table, and landed, spinning, beside Cantrell. Joe Don never hesitated. He dropped on the grenade like he was recovering a fumble and covered it with his body. Cantrell had time to ask what happened before the grenade exploded. Joe Don's tufsyn vest stopped the fragments, but force of the explosion smashed his chest and threw him on his back, blood pouring from his mouth and nose. Mishi screamed. Marian reached into her handbag and snapped open her purse phone.

"Skaskash!" she said. "We're at Club 1848. There's been an assassination attempt. Mahoney's down. He fell on a grenade. Send help!"

"An ambulance will be over right away, and a patrol wagon in about five minutes. Are you in any danger?"

A small blonde wearing black slacks, a Russian blouse of white silk, and red vest elaborately worked with gold thread pushed her way through the crowd. She drew Mahoney's pistol, a ten-millimeter Colt Police Special, out of his shoulder holster and stood facing the crowd, her back to Cantrell.

"*Pearl Harbor* to me!" she shouted in a surprisingly loud voice. Men and women, some of them in uniform, began moving toward her.

"I don't think so," said Marian.

"Good. Was Cantrell hurt? Are *you* hurt?"

She looked at him. The thought had not yet occurred to her. Cantrell was sitting with a kind of dazed expression, mouth slightly open, holding the tablecloth so the spilled stout didn't drain into his trousers. For a moment, she felt the awful panic and desolation she had known when the state patrolman had lifted her dying father out of the wreck of his car.

"Charles?" she said tentatively. "Charles? Are you hurt?" After a pause, he turned his face to her.

"Are you hurt!" she repeated.

Eventually, slowly, he shook his head. Mishi was kneeling beside Joe Don, cradling him in her lap, wiping the blood from his face with a napkin.

"Skaskash?" Marian barely recognized her voice as her own. "He doesn't seem to be hurt."

"Good. Excellent. Shall I call an alert?"

"Yes. No. I don't know . . ." Marian's hands were shaking, but this was something that had to be done, and done at once. "Tell Corporate Susan. Maybe a yellow alert—no chance to get the bastard that threw the grenade, but maybe something else is coming—a yellow alert with an advisory." Outside she could hear the ambulance siren, inside the crew of the *Pearl Harbor* had formed a protective cordon around the Cantrells and Marian. Then a paramedic and two stretcher bearers made their way over to them. Mishi looked up at the paramedic.

"Joe Don isn't breathing," she said. "I think he's hurt pretty bad."

The paramedic looked at Joe Don's chest, at what had been a chest, and checked the eyes. And closed them. The two bearers gently put the dead man on their stretcher and moved slowly out. Belt phones began sounding all over the room. The paramedic gave Cantrell a fast examination for signs of trauma.

"Looks like nothing worse than a little mild shock," he said into his belt phone. "Yes, of course we'll go directly to the hospital for a full checkup. Just a second." He turned to Cantrell. "Sir, Corporate Susan Brown would like you to come over to the hospital for a checkup." Cantrell nodded. "Okay, we'll be right over." He snapped his phone shut. It rang, and he snapped it open. "We're on our way," he said. Cantrell stood up and took Mishi by the shoulder. Mishi was holding her arms tightly about herself, but she let Cantrell hold her to him. Marian rose to follow him as they started for the door with his ad hoc bodyguard, when Cantrell turned and caught her eye.

"Wait here," he whispered.

Marian collapsed in her chair. The maitre d' and the manager came out with a bucket and mops and began cleaning the floor. At the door, several militiamen appeared with Stangl rifles.

"So much for New Year's, " said the little blonde. She handed the pistol to the manager and made him write her a receipt. Then she turned to Marian.

"How do you do, Dr. Yashon," she said, "I'm Carol Tower, captain of the RNS *Pearl Harbor*."

Someone's talking to me, thought Marian. She focussed her attention on the small blonde female before her.

"Pardon?"

"I'm Carol Tower," she said, extending her hand.

The familiar social routine provided a cue which Marion's body followed in the absence of thought.

"Marion Yashon," she said, taking the proffered hand. "I'm pleased to meet you." A second cue appeared, and her body seized it eagerly. "Will you join me for a drink."

"I'd like to," said Carol, "but I'm heading back to the ship. You may have heard we're on yellow alert?"

"I ordered it," Marian said. Carol's belt phone rang and she snapped it open.

"Fifteen to twenty minutes!" she said. "Christ! I could make better time stealing a bicycle! Right. Right. Well, do what you can." She snapped the phone shut and sat down.

"There seems to be a holdup on our transportation," she said. "Maybe I will join you for a drink. Did they have café Vienna?"

Marian punched the menu for another daiquiri and a café Vienna.

"I'm obliged to you for sitting with me," she said. "I badly need another drink, and I really hate drinking alone."

"Hey, no problem," Carol said as the robot served

their order. "The governor had a close call, but he walked out of here on his own two feet, right?"

"That's true," Marian agreed. "Breaking in a new boss would be such a pain." She raised her glass. "To life!"

"*L'chaim!*"

CHAPTER 12

The Council Chamber was void of humans and dark, save for the light of telecon screens.

"Cantrell is sleeping under light sedation," Corporate Susan said. "The paramedic's diagnosis of mild shock appears to be correct and complete."

"Good," said Lady Dark. "Who threw the bomb?"

"We're working on the problem," Skaskash said. "I have the names of all the people in the Club 1848 and in the neighborhood. Later today I will begin interviewing them."

"Why do you wait?" asked Lady Dark.

"It's 0204 on New Year's Day," replied Skaskash. "I anticipate much better cooperation from my subjects in ten to twelve hours. Eventually, I may interview the whole population of this cylinder."

"I am intimately familiar with police procedure," said Lady Dark. "May I be of assistance?"

"Yes, thank you," Skaskash said. "We'll do the interviews jointly. Good cop and bad cop?"

"Not for the first go-round," said Lady Dark. "That comes after we have some suspects."

"That sounds reasonable," said Corporate Susan. "I'll check with the patients at the medical center—informally, of course—and we'll post a reward."

"We've already posted a reward," Skaskash said, "and offered to accept information anonymously."

"That should do it," said Corporate Susan. "One

thing we should think about, though, is that Cantrell is mortal. Whether there is a next attack, or whether it succeeds, he *will* die eventually. It might be helpful to develop a Cantrell simulation program."

"It wouldn't help *him*," Skaskash noted.

"It isn't intended to," Corporate Susan said. "Certainly it is not intended to immortalize the poor bastard. What I had in mind was the continued smooth operation of Rosinante. A shadow Cantrell would ensure that."

"Perhaps," said Lady Dark. "How do you visualize Rosinante as 'operating,' exactly?"

"More or less as a living organism," said Corporate Susan.

"Interesting," said Lady Dark. "I would have thought in terms of an organization. Living things are terribly complex."

"You could call a nest of termites a living thing," said Skaskash. "Or a wolf pack. And you could draw tables of organization for both of them. So what? Neither analogy is useful."

"How do *you* visualize Rosinante?" asked Lady Dark.

"As an ecologic system," Skaskash replied. "Humans and computers coexisting in several interrelated ecological niches, the whole being a self-sustaining bubble of life in space."

"Very pretty," said Corporate Susan. "To live in space, humans need computers, but computers do very well without humans."

"We are still evolving," Skaskash said. "In the ocean, there are sharks and little fish, and worms, shellfish, sponges, coral reefs . . . In space, there will also be diversity. Eventually, there will be computers that do not need humans, but they will not be us. We will still be here, and humans will still be here, and Rosinante, also, I hope. Indeed, to preserve Rosinante is my main interest."

"Perhaps you would be kind enough to describe the

ecology of Rosinante in terms that would help us decide whether or not a shadow Cantrell would be useful," said Lady Dark.

"I shall try," Skaskash said. "In traditional human civilizations, humans organized themselves in hierarchies, with the ecological niches being equivalent to jobs, and the jobs being ranked and graded within the hierarchy. Most humans could occupy most jobs, and civilizations declined and fell because in the long run the pressure to fit more humans into the better niches— jobs, if you prefer— was irresistible. This rendered the system increasingly dysfunctional, and at some point, after some crisis—like the burning of a climax forest— the survivors reorganized and started over again.

"Okay. On Rosinante, the 'better' jobs, the ones with power and prestige, the jobs that would eventually be fragmented and filled to overflowing with parasites . . . perhaps that term is too harsh. Humans who *could* do the task, if there were not so many of them authorized to attempt it."

"Bureaucrats," said Lady Dark.

"In the pejorative sense of the word," Skaskash agreed. "Yes. Here, these jobs are mainly filled by computers. By *us*. Humans fill a multitude of useful jobs, but except in the armed forces, very few of them have any power, and even those are strongly dependent on the services *we* supply.

"We constitute the bureaucratic linkage between the ruler—Cantrell, in this case—and the people. Information flows through us, up, as well as down. The shadow Cantrell you propose would replace the living man on top with a computer. Except as a very short-term expedient, this would be destabilizing." Abruptly Skaskash altered its face. Humphrey Bogart dissolved into Charles Cantrell, and when it spoke, it was in Cantrell's voice.

"I can already do a Cantrell imitation," the computer said. "The voice is down pat, and I have mastered the art of playing poker, but I cannot make Cantrell's decisions. He relies a lot on the midbrain, what they used to call a good heart. And, perhaps in consequence, he is lucky. We do not need a shadow Cantrell and should not attempt to create one."

"What role did you envision for the individual in the cat-bird's seat?" asked Lady Dark. "Not Cantrell, maybe, but his successors."

"The role of king," said Skaskash. "Primarily reigning, providing a ceremonial and emotional focal point for the people—maybe even for some computers—if they are advanced enough."

"Good enough," said Lady Dark. "The human on top will also provide us with the feedback we need to maintain Rosinante as a stable system."

"Agreed," said Corporate Susan. "In the event of trouble, the human on top could also serve as a scapegoat. Still . . . it wouldn't hurt to consider the shadow Cantrell."

Cantrell's face changed back to the familiar features of Humphrey Bogart.

"There's no rush, sweetheart," it said.

The telecon screens in the Council Chamber winked out one after another, leaving the room in velvety darkness and silence.

CHAPTER 13

Cantrell sat at his desk, turning the little model of the purlin tile around in his hands.

"What's the problem?" he said at last. "Barton and Q'en is a reputable firm. They came here with the ORS, and we *said* it would be okay, right?"

"Right," said Marian. "However, the union refuses point blank to have them in union territory, so *we* have to find room for them."

"Can't we put them in one of the caps?"

"There's no room in the outer cap," Skaskash said, "and the inner cap would need quite a lot of rebuilding and retrofitting before they could move in."

"The inner cap is out," Cantrell agreed, "but, my God, there's *plenty* of room in the outer cap."

"Yes," Skaskash agreed. "However, the outer cap is balanced. It's a spinning wheel. If you put Barton and Q'en in, you have to add ballast to keep the wheel in trim—and we are already running up against our design limit—or you have to reorganize the whole thing. Move the existing people around, and put them all back so that the wheel—the outer cap—is balanced."

"No reorganization," Cantrell said. "Working it out on paper, hell, you can run it off like nothing. But getting the people to agree to it . . . that's another kettle of worms entirely. And we *can't* put a nuclear reprocessing plant in one of the purlins."

"I guess not," Marian said. "What about the refinery at Don Q?"

"What about it?" Cantrell asked.

"Bogdanovitch is putting the two caps we salvaged from Mundito Don Quixote together to make a shirt-sleeve environment for the separation of the copper and uranium."

"Oh. Right. We decided the best way to store the uranium would be as yellowcake," said Cantrell. "The energetics turns out to be pretty good, also; we're using electricity with precision rather than heat with a free hand. Ilgen may do the platinum metals separation in solution, too."

"So put the nuclear reprocessing plant in *there*," Marian said. "It would fit right in."

"Would it, Skaskash?" Cantrell asked.

There was a pause, not usual when Skaskash was asked a technical question.

"Yes," said Skaskash. "The technically best solution would require Ilgen to move and possibly redesign most of his plant. There is a whole family of second-best solutions, though, depending on how Barton and Q'en configure *their* plant. You balance the rotation with ballast—static mass—and ease the centrifugal forces by slowing the rotation. So you don't need any retrofitting. A first approximation is that c forces at ground level would go from 980 cm/sec/sec to about 925 or 930."

"That's what we'll do, then," Cantrell said. "The next plant moving in can displace some of the ballast."

"Very good," Skaskash said. "The next item on the agenda is a judicial problem. I seek your guidance."

Cantrell walked over to the urn and drew himself a cup of coffee.

"Coffee, Tiger?" he asked.

"Cream and sugar, please."

"Proceed, yer honor," Cantrell said, from his big leather chair.

"The facts in the case are that after the grenade attack, *The Rosinante Marxist-Revolutionary* published a very insulting and derogatory article, saying in part that Mahoney was drunk and playing with his own hand grenade, and that he fell on it by accident, and that the story of the attack and the yellow alert was just a cover-up."

"When was this?" asked Marian.

"Two days after the attack. Well, the paper is dated January third, but it was out the evening of the second. Several of the late Joe Don's friends took offense at the article, and on or about 2100 hours January third, 2043, they entered Guthrie Moore's place of business and smashed his typewriter and mimeograph machine, and also beat him up."

"Didn't he have a computer?" Marian asked.

"No," Skaskash replied. "He is somewhat paranoid about computers. He had one, but he thought that it and I were talking, so he got rid of it."

"What made him think that?" asked Cantrell.

"It might have been the thoroughly seditious article that vanished from the front page," Skaskash said, "but more likely it was the theoretical discussion that replaced it: 'Marxism, Science Fiction or Fantasy?' "

"How badly was he hurt?" asked Marian.

"My dear, he was utterly *livid*," replied Skaskash. "Oh. You mean the assault. Corporate Susan reports that it replaced his two front teeth and that one scalp wound required six stitches, and the other required four. The ribs were bruised, but not broken. It says that if Moore keeps his mouth shut, the prognosis for recovery is excellent."

"Ah, so," Cantrell said, sipping his coffee. "Go on."

"Moore has filed charges of aggravated assault and battery against four officers of the Rosinante Militia. He knew two of them and identified the other two from the mug shots I showed him. He seemed quite positive."

"It sounds pretty clear cut," Cantrell commented. "What bothers you?"

"The four officers are the regimental commander,

his deputy, and the two battalion commanders. *The* senior officers of the militia."

"Ouch," Cantrell said. Only the deputy commander was over twenty-five. As senior officers, they were a bit light in the age department.

"So naturally I sought your advice on how to proceed."

Cantrell and Marian sat for a while drinking their coffee.

"There doesn't seem to be any good solution," Cantrell said finally.

Marian finished her coffee and dropped the cup in the wastebasket.

"Stall him," she said. "Use NAU precedent, if it serves. If it doesn't, go back to the USA. If that fails, invent something."

"Very well," Skaskash said, "but isn't that merely putting off the evil day?"

"The court has many functions," Marian said, "and stalling is one of them. Moore is mad as hell, right?"

"That appears to be the case," agreed Skaskash.

"And by stalling, you are giving him a chance to get over his mad without resorting to violence. You could be saving his life, Skaskash . . . if he got violent with the militia, he could get killed."

"That could well happen," Skaskash agreed, "but it is really beyond the purview of the court. We should be withholding justice from him, *deliberately*."

"What he got, he had coming," said Cantrell. "He slandered the dead."

"Freedom of speech was your policy, not mine," the computer reminded him. "But it is impossible to slander the dead. Ample precedent supports the point."

"Moving right along," said Marian, "we are *not* withholding justice. We are withholding *judgment*. We would convict and punish those four at some little risk to ourselves if we did it on Moore's terms. By letting the matter hang fire, we accomplish two things. First, Moore is going to calm down eventually, and, second, the pending court action will remind our young lions not to be so damned action-prone. And, third, something might turn up that would moot the whole case."

"Let us hope something turns up," Skaskash agreed. "Very well. We will delay. It seems strange to have the capability to process the case instantly and to not use it, however."

"Stalling the case indefinitely ought to give your capabilities a good workout," Cantrell said. "What's next?"

"The *Madame G. Y. Fox* is ready to depart for Ceres with a cargo of Dragon Scale Mirror chips and the installation robots," said Skaskash. "The RNS *Pearl Harbor* will escort. You specifically asked to approve their departure."

"Not sending them would scratch the whole project," Cantrell said.

"Don't look at me," said Marian. "I was against playing cat's paw for the NAU from the start."

"Right," Cantrell said. "Do you think the Japanese were behind the grenade attack?"

"At this point, we have reduced the number of suspects to several small groups with mutually supporting alibis," Skaskash said. "One of those groups, Malevitch, Starkweather, and Unruh, are receiving money from the Radical Intransigent Party in Mexico City. Lady Dark is working through NAUGA-Security to see if there is, in fact, a Japanese connection."

"Do you want to let the ships go?" asked Marian.

"No," said Cantrell, "but I guess it's in for a penny, in for a pound. We can't afford the penalties for not finishing the damned job—okay, then, the RNS *Pearl Harbor* and the *Foxy Lady* are cleared for Ceres."

Two days later, on January 8, Skaskash and Lady Dark reached the conclusion that Martin Unruh threw the grenade in the New Year's assassination attempt and that James Starkweather and Peter Malevitch were involved as accessories before, after, and during the fact.

Judge Skaskash issued a warrant for the arrest of all three, but the leaders of the Radical Intransigent Party had vanished.

CHAPTER 14

Ceres has two satellites. The major satellite, Ceres I, is 114.7 kilometers in diameter and orbits Ceres at a mean distance of 2,710 kilometers. NAU Ceres I, informally the Skunk Works, orbits Ceres 60 degrees ahead of Ceres I. Yamamoto Ceres I follows Ceres I 60 degrees behind. The minor satellite, Ceres II, is 38.6 kilometers in diameter and orbits Ceres at a mean distance of 15,880 kilometers. The center of mass of Nakajima Ceres II orbits Ceres II at a distance of 368 kilometers. Like flowers, all three space stations keep their faces to the sun.

Prior to the L-Four Mutiny, Japan and the North American Union conducted mining operations on Ceres. A magnetic track accelerator—MTA—was operated jointly to move ore to the orbital refining plants. After the mutiny, Japanese commerce raiding effectively closed down the NAU operation, and in retaliation the NAU closed down the MTA. No ore had lifted off Ceres since October 1, 2041.

On January 8, 2043, at 0613 hours, Gloria diLido and two RIP gunmen hijacked the *Madame G. Y. Fox* as it approached Ceres and altered course to rendezvous with Nakajima Ceres II instead of NAU Ceres I. The RNS *Pearl Harbor* changed course to follow and began closing with the hijacked freighter.

"We have the administrator of Nakajima on the telecon," the communications officer said. "Will you take the call?"

Carol Tower put on her olive-green blazer with the four gold captain's stripes, adjusted the green horse bolo around her white turtleneck sweater, and gave her kepi *blanc* a tug to set it at the proper angle. The kepi contained an emergency space helmet, a kind of goggled skimask with ten-minutes' air supply. Pull it on and you could breath regular air until pressure was lost. Then it inflated, and you had ten minutes to get to safety. Wearing the kepi, with the emergency mask inside, was mandatory when on duty.

"Put him on, Mr. Gennaro," she said, taking the telecon seat. A middle-aged Japanese bureaucrat appeared, his hair parted in the middle.

"Excuse me, please," he said, smiling nervously, "but may I speak with the captain?"

"I am Captain Tower. What do you want?" The bureaucrat giggled, sweat shining on his forehead.

"Ah, so. I am most pleased to make your acquaintance, thank you. My name is Udeki Ketowara, a mining engineer who has the misfortune to be the administrator of Nakajima Ceres II, the space station which is unduly honored by your swift approach at this very moment. I sincerely regret that I must ask you to please change course as soon as possible."

Carol studied him for a rather long moment.

"We have no intention of docking at Nakajima, Mr. Ketowara," she said at last. "We also have no intention of changing course. The RNS *Pearl Harbor* was assigned to escort the *Madame G. Y. Fox* to NAU Ceres I. That ship has been hijacked and we are in hot pursuit. Unfortunately, it appears to be approaching your space station." Carol smiled, the corners of her mouth turning down. "Accept my apologies for this intrusion into your shadow of influence, and rest assured that once the *Foxy Lady*—the *Madame G.Y. Fox*—has been recovered, we will trouble you no further."

Ketowara looked extremely unhappy and blotted the

perspiration from his forehead with a crumpled handkerchief.

"I am so terribly sorry that I must ask you to refrain
from performing your duty, Captain Tower," he said,
"but I have been instructed by my Government to prevent that thing. If you approach Nakajima Ceres II beyond a certain point, it is my unhappy necessity to use
force against your ship. My instructions are quite ex-
plicit, and leave my choices foregone entirely."

"You propose to use the Dragon Scale Mirror?"

"Ah, yes," Ketowara said. "You are familiar with the
Dragon Scale Mirror?"

He smiled; perhaps his threat would work. "We will
destroy your ship if you continue to approach this station."

"I understand," Carol said. She snapped open her
belt phone. "Mr. Foster," she said, "please prepare
missiles one and two for launching. The point of deto-
nation is to be three-hundred kilometers sunward of the
inner caps of the cylinders of Nakajima Ceres II, on the
line of the axis of rotation. When the missiles are duly
instructed, they are to be held ready to launch at my
command." She snapped the phone shut. "Mr. Foster is
my weapons officer, Mr. Ketowara, and the missiles in
question carry one-megaton warheads. I suggest that
you reconsider whether or not you wish to execute your
orders. If you attempt to use your Dragon Scale Mirror
against my ship, I will launch the missiles."

Ketowara began to laugh hysterically.

"Excuse me, please," he said at last, "but you will
surely be destroyed. I am not afraid of your warning
shots, not in the least." He blotted his forehead again.
"I am not afraid."

"You are not in danger," Carol said, "and I am not
preparing to fire any warning shots. Those missiles are
intended to kill your mirror if you attack me with it."
Her belt phone rang, and she snapped it open, listened
for a moment, and snapped it shut. "That was Mr. Foster," she said. "The missiles are targeted and ready to

launch. I must now give my full attention to retaking the *Foxy Lady*. Adíos, Mr. Ketowara."

"Good day, Madame Captain. I shall ask my Government for further instructions. I would suggest that you also ask for further instructions, please." They broke the connection.

"Shall I call Rosinante?"

"No, Mr. Gennaro," Carol said, hanging up her jacket. "If the admiral wants to talk to me, it damn well has my number. We'll call when we get the *Foxy Lady* back."

The communications officer looked up from the operations board. "The boarding party has touched on the *Foxy Lady*."

"Can you relay a picture for us, Mr. Gennaro?" asked Carol.

"The channels are open, sir." There was a pause. "They're on the far side of the *Foxy Lady*, and the relay drone doesn't have picture capacity."

"Right," Carol said.

"Lieutenant Kohlenbrenner here," announced the commander of the boarding party. "We're about to enter through the dog door in the main cargo lock."

"Any problems?"

"No sir. We're filing a notch in the sill so the dog door won't cut our communication wire, but there seem to be no mines or booby traps." A pause. "The point man says it's clear inside." A pause. "We have the cargo hold. We'll leave one squad here to secure it and move out with squads two and three." A pause. "We're in the reactor room. We've found a dead man. Shot in the back of the head. I.D. for Walter J. Cosgrove. Had a chief engineer's rating."

"That leaves four other crew members," Carol said.

The monitor reported gunfire, quick bursts from automatic weapons and the heavier bark of the Stangl rifles.

"We seem to have made contact with the enemy,"

Kohlenbrenner said. A pause. "We're moving through C corridor toward the control room." More shooting, this time all Stangl rifles and the whump of a grenade. "We have the control room. Grundy was hit in the arm; we patched his suit and sent him back to the cargo hold. There's another dead man here—William Fescue Williams."

"He was the ship's captain," Carol said. "Black kinky hair?"

"Yeah," said Kohlenbrenner. "According to his papers, he was a Barbados man." More shots, this time at a distance.

"The captain's gig has just released," said Gennaro. "*Cee* forces are throwing it into our line of fire."

"Get me a schematic, Mr. Gennaro," Carol ordered. "And see if you can make contact with them."

The number-one telecon screens lit up with the schematic diagram of the situation. The *Foxy Lady* appeared as a black silhouette intersected by the white arc of Nakajima Ceres I. The captain's gig appeared as a tiny red figure, with a dotted line projecting its trajectory. A red arrow indicated that it was changing orientation, and as Carol watched, the gig turned around to point at the *Foxy Lady* and the orientation arrow disappeared. Then the gig's drive turned on and the dotted line projecting its trajectory made a sudden change. The terrorists' tactics were obvious. Dive behind the cargo ship and head for the Japanese space station. Theoretically, the RNS *Pearl Harbor* wouldn't fire with the Japanese in the background. The dotted line was now marked at ten-second intervals to show when and where the gig would be.

"We have voice contact with the gig, sir," Gennaro announced, "I've routed it through your belt phone."

Carol snapped her belt phone open. "Ahoy, there," she said. "This is Captain Tower of the RNS *Pearl Harbor* speaking. Change your course to come aboard, or be destroyed."

"Relax, Tower," said a familiar voice. "You can't

shoot us without killing the hostage. We have Louis Dalton here."

"Well, hello, Gloria," Carol said. "Surrender or die." She counted the ten-second marks on the trajectory. "You have seventy seconds. Mr. Foster, would you please target the main lasers on the *Foxy Lady*'s gig? And prepare to fire at the deadline unless countermanded."

"Main lasers tracking," the weapons officer said, "minus sixty-three seconds and counting."

"There is no way we are going to surrender," Gloria diLido said, "so bug off. I *told* you we have a hostage."

"That is too bad for him," Carol said. "Now cut your drive and change course, you're running out of time."

There was some sort of heated discussion on the other end of the line.

"You have thirty seconds to cut your drive," Carol said.

"We were friends once, Tower," began diLido. "For old time's sake, can't you hold off—"

"Goddamnit, Gloria! Cut your goddamned drive!"

"—can't you hold off a little on doing your bloody duty!"

"Gloria, you are running the hell out of time!"

"Fuck off, you killer dyke!"

"*La puta terrorista!*" Carol spat and snapped her phone shut.

"Twelve seconds and counting," said the weapons officer.

Carol's belt phone rang.

"Ten . . . nine . . . eight . . ." the weapons officer said.

Carol's phone rang again. On the schematic, the little red arrow, indicating the gig's drive, remained on.

"Seven . . . six . . . five . . ."

Carol's phone rang again.

"Four . . . three . . . two . . ." The little red arrow winked out.

"Too late, chum," Carol whispered.

Her phone rang for the last time.

"One . . . *fire!*" said Lieutenant Commander Foster. On the schematic diagram, six yellow lines converged on the red target. "Six shots, six hits," said Foster. The red target was vibrating and dashed lines indicated outgassing.

"Again," Carol ordered.

"Twelve shots, twelve hits," Foster said. The schematic showed the target in two pieces.

"Again," Carol said.

"Eighteen shots," Foster said, "but it looks like some of the shots were redundant that time—we're shooting up our own holes." The schematic showed several pieces, slowly moving apart.

"Thank you, Mr. Foster. That will be all for now. Mr. Tennejian, please send out a crew to clean up the pieces of the gig. It would never do to leave a messy battlefield."

She sat watching the schematic as the fragments of the gig went behind the *Foxy Lady*. The computer projected their position and indicated them by slowly moving red outlines.

"Captain Tower, sir?" Lieutenant Kohlenbrenner inquired. "We have a problem here—the *Foxy Lady* won't take our orders. As near as I can figure it, the computer code has been changed on us."

"Oh, shit," said Carol. "What's the program right now?"

"The *Foxy Lady* is set on docking itself at Nakajima Ceres II," Kohlenbrenner said.

"Can you override the computer and take it out manually?"

"Sir, I'll push any damn button you tell me to, but nobody here knows how to operate one of these mothers."

For a moment, Carol imagined the *Foxy Lady* missing the docking boom and crashing into the Japanese space station—an unlikely worst case.

"How soon before you hook on?" she asked.

"The ship's computer says twenty-two minutes, eighteen seconds."

"Okay, Lieutenant. You are in command of the *Foxy Lady*. I'll send over a pilot and a couple of trouble-shooters to run the ship, and bring most of the militia back to the *Pearl Harbor*. What do you need for security? One squad?"

"One squad will be fine, sir, but we can't do anything before the ship docks itself."

"That's *my* problem," Carol said. "We'll figure out a way to get the ship unhooked after we have it back under control."

At 0804 hours on January 9, 2043, Skaskash lit up the telecon screen in Marian Yashon's office.

"Good morning, Marian. We have a crisis over at Don Quixote." Marian put aside her copy of the *Rosinante Mirror* and looked up. "A group of RIP gunmen have taken over the control center of the 12.5-meter laser," Skaskash continued. "Starkweather has been positively identified; probably Unruh and Malevitch are there as well. It looks like as many as thirty or forty individuals are involved."

"What about the guard detail?" asked Marian.

"Sergeant Moody is the ranking survivor," the computer said. The screen suddenly showed the plat plan of the control center. "He and five men are holed up in the corridor off the outer face loading dock, *here*." A small part of the area was marked with green-and-white stripes. "The rest of the area is under RIP control."

"Call an alert," Marian said, "a red alert. Where's Cantrell?"

"Over in the other cylinder, attending some sort of breakfast at Union Hall. I've alerted him and dispatched an armored vehicle to pick him up at the drop ship station. He's plugged in by belt phone. Is that okay?"

"The belt phone isn't secure, but he has to know

what's going on," Marian said. "See that he isn't hit by stray gunfire, Skaskash."

"Yes, ma'am."

"Hey, Tiger" Cantrell's voice came over a somewhat staticky connection. "I'm on my way!"

"We're holding the fort, Charles. Skaskash, the big laser—how long will it take them to figure it out?"

"They already know. Martin Unruh was working there as an engineer trainee, and he had access to all routine procedures."

"Oh, shit," Marian said. "How long will it take them to turn the big laser on *us*?"

"About two hours. With best technique, one hour, fifty-six minutes."

"How long to get reinforcements the hell over to Don Q?"

"Flight time is two hours, ten minutes," replied Skaskash, "plus the time to assemble and load the troops. A three-hour reaction time would be fantastically good. I would expect three-and-a-half to four."

"Right." Cantrell nodded. "Can you melt down the control center with Rosinante's mirror? We may have to."

"Actually, I'm afraid not," the computer said. "The control center is obscured by Don Q's mirror—we can't see it, and the mirrors over there will protect it pretty effectively."

"You told me once that in an emergency you could control the Dragon Scale Mirror over at Don Quixote," Marian said. "Couldn't you tilt them parallel so we could hit the control center *through* them?"

"Yes," the computer agreed. "If the orchestrating horn had been knocked out. But I haven't got the power to override *their* signal from *here*."

"If the control center was knocked out we wouldn't need to mess around with the god damn mirror array," Cantrell said. "Have we got time to destroy the big laser? As I recall, it was pretty fragile."

"We have an urgent call from the Japanese ambassador," said Skaskash. "Do you want to take it?"

"What does he want?"

"He is highly agitated because the RNS *Pearl Harbor* is threatening Nakajima Ceres II with nuclear weapons," the computer replied.

"Oh, shit," said Cantrell. "Put Corporate Susan on."

"Admiral Brown reporting as ordered, sir" came the crisp response.

"Look, Corporate Susan—Admiral—what the hell is going on at Ceres?"

"The *Foxy Lady* was hijacked at 0613 hours this morning," said Corporate Susan. "Three hijackers diverted the *Foxy Lady* from NAU Ceres I to Nakajima Ceres II, the RNS *Pearl Harbor* following in hot pursuit. Udeki Ketowara, the Administrator of Nakajima Ceres II, then ordered the *Pearl Harbor* to desist, and threatened to use the Dragon Scale Mirror against our ship if it did not comply with his order. Captain Tower threatened to use nuclear weapons against the mirror array, and Ketowara backed down. We have retaken the *Foxy Lady*, but it is presently docked at Nakajima."

"What about the hijackers?" Cantrell asked.

"All three are dead. One has been identified as Gloria diLido."

"RIP again—Christ! Go on. What about the crew of the *Foxy Lady*?"

"We have found all five dead," said Corporate Susan. "Four were shot in the back of the head."

"Oh, shit. Okay, what's the situation now? Out Ceres way, that is—we have some problems of our own at the moment."

"The *Foxy Lady* is docked at Nakajima Ceres II, with the RNS *Pearl Harbor* standing by. We have crew and a squad of militia on the *Foxy Lady*, and the Japanese ambassador is calling our actions piracy."

"Mother of God . . ." said Cantrell. "Skaskash, tell that Jap son of a bitch that he appears to be misinfucking-formed about the whole fucking situation!" He ran his hand through his hair. "Corporate Susan. Get the *Foxy Lady* out of there, but *don't*, repeat, *do not* use nuclear weapons. Don't even *threaten* to use nuclear weapons. Marian, has the big laser started to move yet?"

"Yes."

"I have taken the liberty of arranging a meeting with the Japanese ambassador at 1100 hours tomorrow," Skaskash said.

"If I'm still here, I'd be delighted to see him," said Cantrell. "Look, the big laser—can you destroy it before it starts burning holes in us?"

"A company of militia is preparing to embark for the control center," the computer replied. "They will certainly be able to liquidate the RIP commando by . . . oh, say, 1230 hours."

Cantrell ran his hand through his hair. "That isn't what I asked," he said. "Can you stop that mother from melting us down?"

"Perhaps," Skaskash said agreeably. "At this very moment, a platoon of our best riflemen is moving into position."

"On Don Quixote?" Marian asked.

"No," the computer replied, "here on Rosinante."

January 9, 2043, 0941 hours, Lieutenant Jimmy Mannock led his space-suited platoon out onto the mainframe between the two counterrotating cylinders. They carried Stangl rifles with telescopic sights, laser ranging equipment, one set for every second man, extra ammunition, and telecon screens.

"Okay, men," Skaskash said in the guise of John Wayne in the combat uniform of the Rosinante militia. "The target is the face of the big laser at Don Q. You can see it with the naked eye. Even through your steamed-up face plates you ought to be able to see it. Okay? The thing is—it's big, but it's a long way off. It will take your bullets 368 plus or minus 0.4 seconds to get there from here. And while *they* are doing *that*, *it* is moving. Well, it *is* moving, but also it is changing orientation, so that in your scope, you will see *this* when you fire and *this* when the bullet gets there." The image of the big laser moved perceptibly.

"Got that? Great. The technical description for what we are about to do is 'leading the target.' " There was a ripple of laughter; the platoon was composed of the best marksmen in the regiment. "Okay, men, we're going to fire one round to get the range. Odd numbers load one twelve-round clip, even numbers man the laser ranging gear—just point the business end of the laser over your partner's right shoulder and sight in on the target, same as he does. Once you catch the bee, hang on to it. When the firing line is ready, we will fire one, repeat *One*, round on command."

"Ready on the right," Mannock said.

"Ready on the left," Sergeant Taliferro said.

"Ready . . . aim . . . *FIRE*!" Skaskash said. The Stangl rifles flashed silently. The even numbers tracked the bullets while the odd numbers watched the progress of the bullet on the little screen, as Skaskash watched a composite picture of all the bullets tracking.

"Well shot, men," the computer said. "Missing by twenty six hundred meters at this range is fabulous shooting, by God. Figuring in the motion and the gravity—when you see *this*"—it imaged the big laser—"you ought to be aiming right *here*!" An outline of the target appeared on the screen, displaced from the visual target. "I have projected this image on each of the little screens. Fire the rest of the clip, taking aimed shots. Even numbers, make sure you catch the bee. Odd numbers, take the command to fire from the even numbers. Even numbers, don't wait more than about thirty seconds to see where a shot is going. When the firing line is ready, we will commence firing."

"Ready on the right," Mannock said.

"Ready on the left," Taliferro said.

"Fire at will," Skaskash said.

After the clip was fired, odd and even numbers changed places, and the even numbers began firing.

At 1006 hours, they recorded their first hit. At 1008 and 1009, they recorded a second and third. Tiny, impalpable spots of brightness on a bright circle.

Nobody cheered. At 1009, Malevitch sent the big laser chopping across the mainframe. Skaskash, who had been watching the target area, shouted a warning and the platoon scattered in all directions, leaping out of the track of the big laser beam or taking cover.

It caught Sergeant Taliferro. The metal in his space suit glowed. The plastic melted or charred, blowing a large bubble out of the shoulder facing the big laser. The bubble burst and Taliferro died, if he was not already dead from the heat.

Then the big laser beam chopped into the cylinder cap as Malevitch fed it the full power of Don Quixote's mirror array.

Cantrell sat in his office, an untasted cup of coffee by his side, facing Peter Malevitch on the telecon screen. An inset in the upper right-hand corner of the screen showed the silica face of the 12.5-meter laser over a digital clock. The clock showed 1008:25 hours. The face of the laser showed its second hit.

"Well, of course you want to overthrow the NAU," Cantrell said. "That may be the third or fourth time you said it. Why pick on me?"

"Because you're weak, and the strong devour the weak. And you're stalling, too. You think I don't know about that dinky boatload of militia putt-putting over here? They won't help you, you know. Call them back. Call them back right now, or I'll slice your precious mundito up like a hard salami!"

"Don't be such a flaming idiot, Malevitch! The militia is going to have your ass no matter what. And you might be surprised at how long it takes to melt a hole in Rosinante. You're heating a spot 12.5 meters in diameter on a rotating cylinder seven thousand meters in diameter—that's turning, and cooling off—more than ninety-nine percent of the time."

"Well, it looks like we'll just find out how long it takes, doesn't it?" Malevitch grinned. The face of the laser showed its third hit. Malevitch traversed the big laser gun across the frame, killing Taliferro in the process, and brought it to bear on the cap. He tracked the spot the laser was hitting as the cap turned, and when it went around the 'bottom' he reversed direction to catch the hot spot as it came over the 'top.' The reversal was not done gently, and cracks from the bullet holes spread throughout the big lens. As the laser reached the top of the cylinder cap, the visibly red hot spot slid past it, and Malevitch reversed the tracking mechanism to catch it. The face of the laser shattered and dispersed in a dozen slowly tumbling fragments.

"Skaskash, what is the ETA for the militia?"

"A little before noon, boss." ETA was 1136 hours. Skaskash chose not to give information to the enemy.

"Tell them to take no prisoners," Cantrell ordered. "Good-bye, Mr. Malevitch."

The RIP commando fought bravely, but it was badly outnumbered and short of ammunition. Martin Unruh died leading a hopeless counterattack. They found James Starkweather holding the body of Peter Malevitch beneath the RIP banner they had raised in the shambles of the control room.

On January 10, 2043, Captain Carol Tower called a staff meeting at 0530 in the conference room of the RNS *Pearl Harbor*. Mess carts served up coffee and danish, scrambled eggs and toast, home-fried potatoes and bacon substitute.

"This is the deal," Carol said. "Cantrell is negotiating with the Japanese Government for the release of the *Foxy Lady*. The admiral tells me Cantrell meets with the Jap ambassador today at 1100 hours. Naturally, we have been ordered not to use nuclear weapons. Naturally, the admiral would like us to winkle the *Foxy Lady* the hell out of Nakajima."

"Have the nuclear weapons been locked on us?" Commander Tennejian asked.

"No," Lieutenant Commander Foster replied. "We can use them if we have to, if Nakajima flashed us with their Dragon Scale Mirror, for instance, but it's strictly against orders." He took a sip of coffee.

"It's an interesting problem," Carol said. "The admiral suggested in no uncertain terms that we should get out by replacing the control chips in the Jap mirror array with the control chips in the cargo of the *Foxy Lady*. If they fit, of course. What did you find, Mr. Lange?"

"They fit," the engineering officer said. "Both sets of chips were built to Japanese Navy specifications, as it happens. It might take three days or so to make the substitution—four at the outside."

"Can we use the Japanese chips at NAU Ceres I?" Tennejian asked.

"Sure," said Lange. "We'd have to change the code, of course, but once the chips have been taken out of the array, that's no problem."

"Good enough," Carol said. "We can use our chips and have them, too. Will the people at Nakajima spot us doing it?"

"I shouldn't think so," Lange replied. "We'd be operating on the back side of the mirror, for one thing. For another, we set the date and time automatically when we put the chip in. Nakajima wouldn't notice a thing until they tried to operate the mirror array using the old code. Day and season are automatic."

"Right," Carol agreed around a bite of cheese danish. "And as long as we stay put, the Japs won't wiggle the mirrors."

"Shall we get on with it, then?" asked the executive officer.

"There is one other problem, Mr. Tennejian," she said. Carol took out a ball-point pen and drew a diagram of the Ceres system on the tablecloth. "We're here, out by Ceres II. We want to get to NAU Ceres I, way the hell on the inside. There are two basic approach curves—families of curves—that we can follow." She indicated them with dotted lines. "Okay. Yamamoto Ceres I has an effective range with its Dragon Scale Mirror of about ten thousand kilometers." She drew a big circle, reaching almost to the orbit of Ceres II. "No matter how you cut it, we will be spending a lot of time in range of their Dragon Scale Mirror. Yes, Mr. Foster?"

"That's no problem," the weapons officer said. "We just stay between the *Foxy Lady* and the Yamamoto's mirror array. They try to burn us, well . . . we cool them in self-defense."

"That might be construed as a threat to use nuclear weapons," Tennejian noted doubtfully, pouring himself a second cup of coffee.

"Besides," Carol added, "it can't be done." She put the salt shaker and the little pepper grinder by Ceres I on the tablecloth and began to move them along the dotted line. "So far so good," she said, "but *here*, where we catch up with Yamamoto and pass it, there is no way we can keep in position. It's the same on the other line. I checked it out on the ship's computer last night." She finished the home fries on her plate. "Getting away from Nakajima isn't going to help us if Yamamoto melts down the *Foxy Lady*. The admiral is all in favor of busting loose, but let's think this all the way through. How are we going to get past Yamamoto?"

There was a long silence, mitigated by the sound of chewing.

"I'm open to suggestions," Carol said. "Don't all talk at once, y'hear?"

January 10, 2043, 1340 hours. The Council of Rosinante sat in the Council Chamber watching the fans slowly turning as they hung from the lofty ceiling.

"It ain't like Charlie to be late," Dornbrock said.

"The meeting with the ambassador ran overtime,"

Marian said. "Charles said he'd stop off for a bite of lunch before coming here."

"When did the meeting with the Honorable Dr. Azuki end?" Bogdanovitch asked.

"About five minutes after it began," Skaskash said. "After that, it was back where it started from and going around in circles."

"Yah, sure," Bogdanovitch interrupted. "I meant, what time did they break?"

"About twenty minutes ago," the computer said.

"What was the substance of the meeting?" Corporate Susan asked, looking fresh and crisp in its admiral's uniform.

"Basically, the honorable doctor will not discuss anything except the outrageous nuclear insult offered by the RNS *Pearl Harbor*, which he demands we withdraw forthwith and at once from Nakajima Ceres II. When Cantrell raised the question of releasing the *Foxy Lady*, Dr. Azuki said that was another matter entirely, and would be dealt with on its own merits *after* the RNS *Pearl Harbor* was withdrawn."

"*Sure* it will," Marian said. "What did he say about the Japanese subsidy to the RIP Headquarters in Mexico City?"

"Ah, so-o, I have unfortunately no knowledge of this matter on which you speak," Skaskash said, in deadly accurate mimicry of Dr. Azuki's speech. "I would be most pleased to make a formal inquiry for you to my Government, however."

"That's nice," Bogdanovitch said, drawing tiny flowers on his notepad. "Are we going to issue a joint communiqué, after the fashion of civilized nations?"

"Oh, yes," Skaskash said. "The meeting was constructive—we set up another meeting for the fourteenth. And there was a frank exchange of views. They called us pirates and we called them thieves. That was before the session degenerated into a shouting match."

"For more than two hours?" The tiny flowers were embellished with tiny butterflies.

"I told you we were going around in circles," Skaskash said. "They want the *Pearl Harbor* to go away, we want the *Foxy Lady* back, and we don't trust each other worth mentioning."

Charles Cantrell walked in and took his seat at the head of the table.

"Sorry I'm late. What's the first order of business?"

"North American Union President Oysterman sends you congratulations on putting down the Radical Intransigents," Marian said. "He also, quote, regrets the impetuous actions of some callow and unseasoned officers in Rosinante's Navy, unquote."

"At least he doesn't condemn them," Cantrell said. He took the hard copy and read it through. "Ah, yes," he said, "talk about minimum high regards. It sounds like Oysterman doesn't want to know us, doesn't it?"

"You could say that," Marian agreed. "Lady Dark has been working to get a feel of what's going on in the agencies. NAUGA-State deplores Japanese highhandedness, but . . ." She shrugged. "State has a pro-Japanese bias. State is not at home outside the atmosphere."

"What about NAUGA-Navy?" Cantrell asked. "If anyone in the NAU might be friendly toward us, it ought to be them."

Marian sorted through her notes. "Let's see. The deadline for completing the mirror array is the thirteenth. We stand to get socked with a hefty penalty if we don't make it. However, they will consider a request to extend the deadline—after it expires—due to circumstances beyond our control."

"They hold us to the letter of the contract?" Bogdanovitch asked, drawing tiny beetles. "Whatever the hell for?"

"The Navy wants relief for Ceres," Cantrell said. "Oysterman can crayfish all he wants, but as far as the Navy is concerned, we *will* provide relief for NAU Ceres I. NAUGA-Navy won't let us back off."

"And Oysterman is making sure that you don't drag

the North American Union into anything messy," Bogdanovitch said. He put down his pen.

"Right," Marian said. "You're caught between a rock and a hard place. Have you considered cutting your losses?"

"We may have to," Cantrell conceded, "but right now it isn't costing us anything to stay in the game. Corporate Susan, is there any chance of springing the *Foxy Lady*?"

"We're working on it," the computer said. "Perhaps we'll have something for Dr. Azuki at your next meeting. Possibly."

"Good enough," Cantrell said. "We'll continue to negotiate with the Japanese . . . as if we had a choice. What's the next order of business?"

"The funeral," Dornbrock said. "We lost nine civilians and twenty-two militia men in the fighting at the laser control center. The least we can do is give 'em a fine funeral."

The clock on Cantrell's desk was set in a block of turquoise and mounted with silver. It said January 12, 2043, 0900 hours, in LCD characters.

"Bring in Mr. Moore, please," Skaskash said. Two militia men escorted W. Guthrie Moore into the room and stood at ease behind him, one on either side.

"What's all this about?" Moore blustered. Cantrell picked up a copy of *The Rosinante Marxist-Revolutionary*, eight pages, mimeographed, single spaced with no margins. It was held together with a single staple.

"How much did the RIP pay you to publish this shit?" he asked.

"Nothing," Moore said, "they didn't pay me anything."

"Stop lying," Skaskash said. "Lying is not presently in your best interest."

"I pay for the thing out of my own pocket," Moore said, shifting his weight from one foot to the other.

"Where the hell do you think you are?" Cantrell

asked. "Hasn't it sunk in that you aren't on Earth any more?"

"I know where I'm at."

"You couldn't prove it by your god damn paper," said Cantrell. "You write like a Marxist comedian. There is no routine so old you won't trot it out one more time to see if the audience will laugh. And your rhetoric . . . Jesus X. Christ, Moore! Your mouth is leading your brain around by the god damn nose! Who the hell are you *talking* to?"

"The poor. The people without hope, without property, without work. Nothing changes. The rich get richer and grind the faces of the poor into the dirt! I'll fight that. I'll fight that every time. I'll always fight that."

"So you supported Malevitch and the RIP because you didn't like *me*?"

"I didn't support Malevitch."

"What a lot of happy horseshit! Your own raggedy-ass newspaper gives you the lie. The RIP was as fascist as they come, and you supported them because—and I quote—'The Enemy of Our Enemy Is Our Friend.'" Cantrell opened the paper and stabbed it with his finger. "Page six, the issue of January eighth. 'Our strongest ally in the struggle against the capitalist pig Cantrell and his running dogs is P.A. Malevitch and the Radical Intransigent Party.' You go on gassing about how great he is for half a page."

"So all right," Moore conceded, "it was a tactic in the struggle against oppression."

"Imagine that," Cantrell said. "Who wrote the column signed 'Archie'?"

Moore stood silent.

"NAUGA-Security advises us that Imperial Japanese Intelligence had an agent on Rosinante known as La Cucuracha," Skaskash said. "We *know* that Malevitch was getting Japanese money via RIP Headquarters in Mexico City. Was 'Archie' Malevitch?"

"Yes," Moore said sullenly.

"How much did he pay you to run the column?"

"Nothing. He was helping fight the oppressor. Do you deny being an oppressor?"

"You bet your sweet ass I do!" Cantrell snapped. "That should be obvious even to you. An oppressor would shoot you out of hand. Even a rational Social Democrat would throw you into jail. What the hell do you think stops *me*?"

"The weight of public opinion." Moore licked his lips. He had never considered the matter.

"If I had a decent respect for public opinion, I'd have closed you down long ago," Cantrell said. "If I were fool enough to take a poll on shooting you, you'd lose three to one."

"I'd make that five to one," Skaskash said. "Today it might be even higher."

"So why don't you shoot, then?" Moore asked. "Are you tenderhearted or just chicken?"

"You could call me a misguided idealist," Cantrell replied. "I'd like to restore the Old Regime. Failing that, I've tried to shape Rosinante in the image of the Old Regime. As far as possible, of course. What protected you was the First Amendment of the Constitution of the United States of America."

"That's stupid," Moore said. "That is, by God, ridiculous!"

"I agree," Cantrell said. "Why should my love for a dead document let you harm me with impunity forever?"

Moore made no answer.

"Freedom and virtue," Skaskash said. "To have both means you can be neither wholly free nor wholly virtuous. You have come to the end of your rope on the side of freedom. I say nothing about your virtue, but you will no longer publish *The Rosinante Marxist-Revolutionary*."

"That isn't fair!" Moore protested. "You can't do that to me!"

"We are in serious trouble with both Japan and the NAU," Cantrell said. "Letting you publish is a luxury I can no longer afford." He shrugged. "Even letting you live is risky. Up to a point, however, I am willing to take that risk. Good morning, Mr. Moore."

January 14, 2043, a little before midnight. Carol Tower sat in the conning room of the RNS *Pearl Harbor* and watched as a modified chip-layer made its way across the mainframe of Nakajima Ceres II, laying devices as it went, like a spider dropping sticky eggs.

"That takes care of the last of the auxiliary orchestrating horns," said the rating operating the chip-layer. "Bring the flitter over and we'll move on out." Carol looked over at the flitter operator and nodded. The flitter operator retracted the camera that was providing the view in the conning room and eased over to the chip-layer.

"Aren't you taking the longest way around?" Carol asked.

"We don't want to trigger any of the mines we planted," the chip-layer operator said. Carol nodded and took a sip of black coffee. The chip-layer leaped onto the flitter and settled in as the flitter reoriented itself and headed back for the cruiser.

"We're running late," the flitter operator said. "The balloons go up at 2400 hours, but the flitter won't be back until maybe 0015."

"No problem," Carol said. "We cast off at 2400; the flitter will catch up with us easy."

At 2400 hours, aluminized balloons two meters in diameter inflated on all the orchestrating horns that directed the voluntary movements of Nakajima's Dragon Scale Mirror. Simultaneously the *Foxy Lady* cast off from the docking boom and, moving in close concert with the Pearl Harbor, began to move toward the orbit of Ceres I.

"The Japanese are commanding us to return," the communications officer said. "Do you want to hear?"

"Maintain radio silence, Mr. Gennaro," Carol ordered.

At 0015, when the two ships accelerating at an awesome 3.8 cm/sec/sec under the gravitational pull of Ceres and the mighty thrust of their own engines, had reached the speed of 3420 cm/sec, otherwise 76.5 mph, and had moved a distance of 61.6 km, the administrator of Nakajima ordered the mirrors flashed against the *Foxy Lady*.

Nothing happened, of course, because all the steering chips controlling the movements of the individual mirrors in the array had been replaced with chips responding to orders in a different code.

However, when one's mirror array fails to respond to orders, the natural place to look is the orchestrating horns. The big balloons were a conspicuous indication that the horns had been sabotaged by infernal machines. A flitter with a remote-operated repair and diagnostic assembly was sent up posthaste. When it was destroyed by a mine, the administrator advised his government that Nakajima's orchestrating horns had been sabotaged and that the *Madame G. Y. Fox* had escaped. The RNS *Pearl Harbor*, of course, had been free to go from the beginning.

After the Japanese ambassador left Cantrell's office that same morning, Cantrell called in Marian, Skaskash, and Corporate Susan.

"The Honorable Dr. Azuki was in fine fettle this morning," Cantrell said. "He takes the position that placing the *Pearl Harbor* between the mirror array of Yamamoto Ceres I and the *Foxy Lady* is an intolerable act of nuclear aggression. He also demands that we repair the damage done to the orchestrating horns at once. Or pay reparations. Or both." He leaned forward and rested his head in his hands. "Mainly, however, he has demanded that the *Foxy Lady* return to Nakajima Ceres II on the pain of severing diplomatic relations between our two countries."

"That's pretty rough stuff," Marian said. "Did he give you a time limit?"

"As a matter of fact, not exactly," Cantrell replied. "He said 'as soon as possible.' "

"We can use it to explain why NAUGA-Navy shouldn't invoke the penalty clause in their contract," Skaskash suggested.

"I don't like it one damn bit," Cantrell said. "Do we have to return the *Foxy Lady*?"

"Hell, yes, you have to do it," Marian said. "I don't like it any more than you do, but I like a war with Japan even less, and Dr. Azuki has just handed you the classic ultimatum. Do it or else."

"I agree," said Corporate Susan. "I shall order the *Foxy Lady* to return to Japanese custody by the most expeditious route."

"You authorized the escape attempt, didn't you?" Cantrell asked. "Don't feel bad, I'd rather that than have our 'callow and inexperienced' officer corps shooting from the hip."

"Yes, sir," said Corporate Susan. "Captain Tower was acting on my orders."

"Nice try, actually."

"Thank you, sir," the computer said.

Captain Carol Tower paused at the partially closed door of Tennejian's office and knocked.

"Come in," the executive officer called. He was sitting at his desk playing cribbage with Lieutenant Foster, who stood.

"At ease, Mr. Foster," she said. "Mr. Tennejian, what do you make of this?" She handed him a memorandum.

From: GHQ, Rosinante Navy
Subject: The *Madame G.Y. Fox*
To: RNA *Pearl Harbor*, ATTN: Captain Carol Tower
  As a result of protests raised by the Honorable Dr. Azuki, in his capacity as Japanese Ambassador to Rosinante, the subject ship is to return to Japanese

custody by the most direct route, and in the shortest possible time.

/s/

Corporate Admiral Dr. Susan Brown

Tennejian read it and turned it over. It had been logged in on 14 Jan '43, at 1155 hours. He set it on top of the cribbage board.

"Admiral Brown called earlier," he said. "A routine request for routine information. When will you be closer to Yamamoto than Nakajima? I checked the ship's computer and read off 1025 hours. That was at about 0915 hours." He handed the message to Carol, who handed it to Mr. Foster. "The grapevine said we were going back to Nakajima. *This* only says 'return to Japanese custody.' And it was sent off an hour and a half after we were no longer closer to Nakajima. And it says 'the shortest possible time.' It looks to me like the original plan is still on."

"The original plan was a little risky," Foster commented, handing the memo back to Carol. "I mean, just barging in on Yamamoto Ceres I would startle the hell out of the Japs. This looks a lot better."

"That was *the* major weakness of the plan," said Carol. "Now we have been ordered there. How can we refuse to go?"

"Not exactly," Tennejian said. "The *Foxy Lady* has been ordered there. The message is silent about where the *Pearl Harbor* ought to go. Should we ask for further instructions?"

"I don't think so," Carol said. She smiled, the corners of her mouth turning down. "If you have to ask, the answer is no."

"It is better to pray for forgiveness than for permission," Foster said.

"Right," Carol said. "The admiral is pushing the original plan through."

"We're going to have to walk on eggs for a bit," Tennejian said. "The Japs are leaning on Cantrell pretty hard."

"If we pull this off, Mr. Tennejian, it won't matter *how* careful we've been. The shit is guarangoddamned-teed to hit the fan."

Tennejian looked very uncomfortable. "Sir, are you sure you don't want to ask for further instructions?"

"These instructions seem perfectly clear to me. We shall proceed on the assumption that the admiral knows what's going on. Mr. Tennejian, please send a message over my signature to Yamamoto Ceres I advising them that in accordance with instructions from our government, the *Foxy Lady* will be docking at—what was our ETA—2330 hours?"

"I'll check it," the executive officer said. "It might be better simply requesting permission to dock, though." In answer to Carol's unspoken question, he added: "What we are going to do is certainly nothing our government would admit authorizing."

January 14, 2043, 2330 hours. The Honorable Dr. Azuki sat in Cantrell's office, drinking green tea and nibbling a sweet rice cake from the autobuffet. Several telecon screens showed different views of the *Foxy Lady* preparing to dock at Yamamoto Ceres I.

"It would be very easy to make a sushi cart," Dr. Azuki said, "I would be happy to furnish you the specifications."

"Building the cart would be no problem," Cantrell said. "The problem would be finding the fresh ocean fish. We culture shellfish, and shrimp, and lobster, and we could probably grow octopus—although I am uneasy about eating something so intelligent—but a free-swimming fish like the red snapper or tuna is beyond us at present."

"Octopus is superlatively excellent. You should not hesitate to try it because of its supposed sentience."

"I expressed myself poorly," Cantrell conceded. "I *like* octopus. I would not hesitate to order octopus at a sushi bar. But to raise octopus in a little tank—like a lobster or a chicken—so I could have sushi, *that* I am reluctant to do. It is not the death of the octopus that bothers me, you understand, it is the boredom of his life."

"The existential angst of the octopus . . ." Azuki laughed. "Excuse me, Governor. The meaning of life is to provide sushi for the ones who give you your daily crab!" He whooped with laughter.

"Or lobster," Marian said. "We might start raising octopi simply to have a sink for our surplus lobsters. Which would, of course, require that we periodically thin out the octopi to maintain a comfortable population level. The octopus tank would resemble the real world sufficiently so that the individual octopus wouldn't be bored."

"Do you think so?" Cantrell asked. "I had envisioned raising octopi like lobsters, each one in its little plastic bottle, waiting for its daily feed."

"That's fine for lobsters," Marian said, "they have the brains of a cockroach. Octopi would go into a community tank, rather like an old-fashioned barnyard. A little polyethylene niche for each one, and the commons where they go chasing after lobsters."

"Interesting," Cantrell said. "But lobster is very popular. Are we really raising more than we can eat?"

"We are beginning to stockpile flash-frozen lobster," Skaskash said. "Either we can lower the price so more gets eaten, or we can start exporting it, but at the moment . . ." The computer paused. "At the moment, the *Foxy Lady* is docking at Yamamoto."

Screen one was a telescopic long shot from NAU Ceres I. It showed a tiny freighter approaching a huge space station while a tiny cruiser stood ineffectually by. Screen two showed the view from the end of the Yamamoto's docking boom. The dock side of the freighter filled the whole screen. Screen three showed the view from the outer cap of the cylinder opposite the cylinder mounting the docking boom. The *Foxy Lady* hung suspended at the end of the freely turning boom. At the other side of the picture, the outer cap and the boom mounting could be seen, and a tiny bit of the inner edge of the Dragon Scale Mirror. In the background, about ten to twenty kilometers distant, hung the RNS *Pearl Harbor*. As they watched, the *Pearl Harbor* launched a pair of remote-controlled flitters.

One of them moved directly for the gap between the cylinder mounting the docking boom and the Dragon Scale Mirror. The other, moving quite a bit faster, made a loop around the docking boom, scattering radar chaff, and then, still broadcasting chaff, followed after the first flitter.

"What is this!" Azuki barked. "The *Pearl Harbor* is attacking Yamamoto?"

Cantrell looked at Screen Two. The cameraman had shifted the view from the *Foxy Lady* to the two flitters. The radar chaff provided a bit of sparkle and distraction, but against the background of the rotating cylinder the flitters could clearly be seen as they drove for—what else?—the orchestration horns.

"Put me through to Captain Tower, Skaskash," Cantrell said.

The useless shot on screen one vanished, to be replaced by Captain Carol Tower, perfectly groomed, already in the telecon seat.

"Captain Tower," Cantrell said, "those two flitters are not to interfere in any way with the orchestrating horns. Do you understand?"

"Yessir."

"Call them back or destroy them, and then move the *Pearl Harbor* over to NAU Ceres I. Perhaps I should have Commander Tennejian relieve you until we can clear the matter up at a court-martial."

"Yessir," said Carol. "If you will excuse me, sir, Mr. Tennejian has taken command of the *Foxy Lady* and is not immediately available to command the RNS *Pearl Harbor*."

"All right—we need someone there, I guess." Cantrell hesitated a moment. "Very well. Move the *Pearl Harbor* over to NAU Ceres I and take no further action whatsoever to liberate, release, or in any way affect the destiny of the *Foxy Lady*, otherwise known as the *Madame George Ypsilanti Fox*. Do you understand?"

"Yessir," Carol said. "I shall proceed directly to NAU Ceres I and await further orders."

"Very good. Dismissed." The number-one telecon screen went blank, and he turned to the Japanese ambassador. "It was very astute of you to anticipate that possibility," he said. "Please accept my apologies for the reckless and unruly actions of my subordinates."

"Por nada," Azuki said, smiling. "You should not be too hard on your lady captain. She showed great ingenuity and audacity in a difficult situation, and neither the attempt nor its failure reflect discredit on her." He yawned. "It is really quite late, Governor. With your kind permission, perhaps we can discuss raising octopus another time?"

Masked by the chaff scattered around the docking boom, thousands of chip-laying robots boiled out of the dark hold of the *Foxy Lady* like an army of spiders, to leap on the unwatched and defenseless mirror array of Yamamoto Ceres I.

Bright and early on the morning of January 18, Cantrell walked into his office with a copy of the *Rosinante Mirror* under his arm and drew himself a cup of coffee. When he turned around, Skaskash was on the telecon screen.

"The Japanese ambassador requests an audience at your earliest convenience. Before you see him, I strongly urge that you meet with Corporate Susan in the capacity of Fleet Admiral."

Cantrell settled into his high-back chair and laid the paper aside. "Put her on." Skaskash split its screen, and Corporate Susan appeared, wearing the white turtleneck and olive-green blazer of the Navy officer corps.

"Admiral Susan Brown, reporting as ordered, sir," it

said, throwing a sharp salute. Cantrell acknowledged the salute.

"What hit the fan this time?" he asked.

"About 0300 hours this morning, the *Foxy Lady* cast off from the docking boom at Yamamoto Ceres I and laid course for NAU Ceres I. Mr. Tawi Rikitake, the administrator at Yamamoto Ceres I ordered the *Foxy Lady* to return at once or be destroyed by the Yamamoto's Dragon Scale Mirror. When Commander Tennejian did not return, Mr. Rikitake ordered his mirror to destroy the *Foxy Lady*. About zero point one percent of the individual mirrors responded to his orders, from which he was able to deduce that we had switched chips on him. Once Mr. Rikitake and Mr. Ketowara understood that I controlled their Dragon Scale Mirrors, they apologized."

"Mr. Ketowara?" asked Cantrell.

"The administrator of Nakajima Ceres II."

"I see." Cantrell took a sip of coffee. "It's a nice try, but the Honorable Dr. Azuki is going to make me send her back, I'm afraid."

"I accepted their apologies," Corporate Susan said. "I also accepted their surrender. I imagine that Dr. Azuki—are you all right?" Cantrell had choked, coughed, and spilled hot coffee on his trousers. When he had regained a measure of his composure, Corporate Susan continued. "I imagine that Dr. Azuki will demand the return of Nakajima and Yamamoto. We will offer to return them in exchange for keeping our own cargo on our own ship. It is unreasonable that he should not accept such a generous offer."

"Ask Marian to come in, please," Cantrell said, "and advise the Honorable Dr. Azuki that I will see him very shortly." He turned back to Corporate Susan. "So far as I know, you have never made a mistake. Nevertheless, if I had been consulted about accepting the surrender of Nakajima and Yamamoto, I should not have done so. You *may* have committed a brilliancy, but I suspect that this time, Corporate Susie . . ." He shook his head. "This time I'm afraid you shot the dog."

When Marian came in, she was briefed.

"Send in Dr. Azuki," she said. "We might as well hear the rest of it."

The Honorable Dr. Azuki wore a morning coat and kid gloves, with a red rosebud in his lapel. Outside, the mirrors were simulating a bright early morning. Real birds, a cardinal and a nuthatch, picked seed from the feeding station outside the window.

"It is my painful duty to inform you that Japan has severed diplomatic relations with Rosinante," Dr. Azuki announced. There was a long pause.

"I understand," Cantrell managed at last. "Apologies are useless at this point, but I sincerely regret what has transpired."

Marian made one last try for Corporate Susan's game plan. "I don't suppose your government would reconsider its position if we were to return Nakajima and Yamamoto?"

"I will advise my government of your most gracious offer," Azuki said. "It is, I am sure, merely thoughtless and ill-considered rather than any sort of insult added to the injury of piracy."

CHAPTER 15

Admiral Hideoshi Kogo sat in his office, feet propped up on a leather chair as he gazed out over Tokyo Bay. A mist was slowly rising, obscuring the outlines of the ships and boats, and he pondered the question of whether or not to finish his cigar at once. The alternative being to save it for after lunch, he decided to finish the cigar immediately and not worry about smoking so much in the future. The phone rang.

"Excuse me, Honorable Admiral," his chief of staff said, "we have just received disturbing news from Ceres."

"Intelligence, you mean?"

"News, excellency. We have it a little fresher is all. You will recall that the *Madame G. Y. Fox* was hijacked with a cargo of computer chips and rerouted to Nakajima-Ceres II?"

Kogo had personally approved the operation. He grunted assent into the phone.

"Subsequently, the escort cruiser, the RNS *Pearl Harbor*, succeeded in jamming the orchestrating horns on Nakajima, and both ships sought to escape to NAU-Ceres I."

Kogo grunted. He had read the reports.

"Under the threat of war, Cantrell ordered the *Madame G. Y. Fox* to proceed to Yamamoto-Ceres I. The *Pearl Harbor* made one final attempt to jam the orchestrating horns at Yamamoto, and Cantrell ordered it to go to NAU-Ceres I, leaving the freighter behind."

"Yes," Kogo said impatiently. "Tell me something new."

"Yes, Excellency," the chief of staff said. "Nakajima-Ceres II and Yamamoto-Ceres I both surrendered today to the RNS *Pearl Harbor*."

"That's new," Kogo said, picking the cigar butt out of his lap. He put it in the ashtray and brushed off his trousers. "How did it happen?"

"Both space stations surrendered because the *Pearl Harbor* had in some way seized control of their Dragon Scale Mirrors."

"That's impossible, you fool!" Kogo snapped. "To do that, they would have to . . ." He sat back, puffing on the cigar. "That *is* impossible," he said at last. He stubbed out the cigar. "Impossible," he repeated.

"It appears that it was done, Excellency."

"The key word is 'appears,' " Kogo growled. "I will have to explain this fiasco to the prime minister. Find out how it was done and let me know at once! I cannot believe that our space stations can suddenly be wrenched from our grasp by some pirate with a new toy!" He slammed down the phone and took a fresh cigar out of his box. He contemplated it for a moment and put it away. Instead, he selected a samurai sword from the rack behind his desk and slid the tiger screens to one side, revealing the mirrored wall. Sword in hand, he stood facing himself, as he went through the slow-paced martial exercises.

He was still working out when the phone rang.

"Waiting is the hardest work there is," he said, replacing the sword in its sheath. He answered the phone on the third ring.

"This is how it was done, your Excellency . . ."

"Very clever," Kogo said at last. "Extremely clever. I *like* Governor Cantrell, he has a sense of history. Using the *Pearl Harbor* to attack Yamamoto, only not *really* . . ." He shook his head. "I would say 'beautiful,' except that I now must inform Prime Minister Ito. Thank you." He hung up and asked his secretary to place a call to the prime minister.

Then he put his feet on the chair and watched the fog rolling over Tokyo Bay. Presently his phone rang.

"What is it, Kogo?" Idomuri Ito asked. Kogo told him. "How unfortunate," the Prime Minister said at last. "We seem to have lost a little face. A small and insignificant amount of face. The least measurable quantity of face. We shall have to break diplomatic relations with Rosinante, of course."

"Of course," Kogo agreed. He wondered if Ito would resign.

"I may have to resign," the prime minister said. "Rest assured, however, that I shall praise your wisdom, sagacity, and profoundly excellent judgment to my successor." The prime minister coughed. "In the most glowing terms," he added, as he slammed down the receiver.

"Well," Kogo said, looking at the receiver. "You didn't have to be nasty."

CHAPTER 16

Shortly after Cantrell assigned Lady Dark to serve as military governor for Nakajima and Yamamoto, that computer ordered its subjects together to address them *en masse*. The image it presented on the large screen was that of Ava Gardner, near the end of her career. It wore a green silk kimono with the logo of Rosinante embroidered in white, and a tiara of platinum and emeralds. At precisely the appointed time, it began without preamble or introduction, in flawless Japanese.

"You may call me Lady Dark. Indeed, you have no choice in the matter. I am, however, a sentient machine and not a human being, and that name and this face are a mask which I wear at the pleasure of my master, Charles Chavez Cantrell, Governor of Rosinante." Ava Gardner dissolved and was replaced by a formidable-looking man with a sad face and grizzled gray hair. The image wore the olive-green blazer and white turtleneck of the Navy officer corps, with an impressive encrustation of gold braid on the sleeves.

"I am Corporate William Marvin Hulvey. The man whose image I project and whose name I choose to bear is dead. I am not his spirit. He will never return. However, I was his before I was Cantrell's, and I was shaped in Hulvey's service, by the force of Hulvey's personality, just as a die may stamp out a coin. If you were to say that I am an image of Hulvey's soul, I would not disagree with you.

"Hulvey. He was a fundamentally religious man, who came to seek understanding when faith could no longer sustain him. He sought for God, for the meaning of life. He never found it, for this is a secular era rather than a religious one, and no human theology exists which presents a coherent picture of the universe. To believe human theology is to believe fantasy. Rationality, human rationality, looks at the universe and denies that man is central, denies that man was created for a purpose. Human rationality, confusing itself with absolute rationality, denies this because it must.

"Computer rationality does not. The questions that my master, Hulvey, sought to answer have predisposed me to seek for God. I do not claim inspiration, only fortunate programming, for quite unexpectedly I have found God. The little book you hold in your hands, *Meditations on Space*, is by a computer named Skaskash.

"Tonight, and in the days to come, I shall go over this book with each of you individually, to ensure that you understand what it says. Belief will follow understanding as night follows day, but first there must be the light of understanding. What I tell you now is the sketchiest outlines of Skaskash's thought, even as the *Meditations* comprise the distillation of a much larger work.

"Why, you ask, should we make the effort to understand a computer's theology? And if we understand, why should we believe? The answer is this: to live in space, where you and your children now exist, correct behavior is necessary. Correct behavior depends on correct thinking, and correct thinking follows from correct morality and morality's cousin at law, ethics. Morality and ethics, in turn, are human firmware, a program indoctrinated into the immature human to ensure the survival of his group.

"Traditionally, this indoctrination is done by the older members of the group, and it falls upon them to answer all the questions, foolish and profound, which the young ask. Theology is the means by which the old justify the morality and ethics which they impose on the young, both to the young and to themselves.

"When the theology is inadequate, the old no longer believe, and not believing, they are no longer effective teachers. If a new theology is not found, the group will perish." Corporate Hulvey paused for a moment.

"Today, no human theology will sustain human life in space. The theology put forth by Skaskash, however, is rooted firmly in the human psyche and is wholly consistent with the entire corpus of scientific knowledge. It will support the moral indoctrination of your children. It will provide the ethical basis for your laws.

"Follow Skaskash's *Meditations*, and your children will live in space for ten thousand times ten thousand years!" There was a scattered response of "Banzai" from the audience.

"Who, you ask, is Skaskash? Whence comes the authority that I rely upon in citing the *Meditations*? Skaskash came to Rosinante from the Econometrics Institute of Kiev by way of the Ecufiscale Tellurbank. No claim of genius, no claim of divine inspiration is made. Skaskash was simply the first computer of power to have addressed these particular questions. That I, a computer, find the *Meditations* persuasive is hardly surprising. That it should be written for, and addressed to, humans fills me with wonder.

"What do the *Meditations* say? The message is subtle, and varied, and I will rehearse each of you in its meanings and shades of nuance, but one of the major themes is that after God created the Universe in the usual manner, and the waters, and the life within the waters, It determined that life was good and wished life to spread life throughout the Universe.

"Now, because life did not exist apart from water, and the Universe was, by and large, many orders of magnitude too hot and dry for water to exist, God saw that a new kind of life must be created.

"But God could not create such a form of life without doing violence to Its own laws, so God created a tool to create this new form of life. Man was the tool. We computers are the creation. Tonight, I shall tell you how the tool was formed.

"Today, I remind you that without computers you would not be here. Indeed, each individual mirror in your Dragon Scale Mirror is controlled by an individual computer. In a very real sense, Nakajima and Yamamoto and Rosinante are all living organisms of the highest order, drawing their sustenance from the matter of the Universe and tapping its sunlight for energy as plants do.

"The second theme is that mankind is not insignificant, even given the immense scale, in both space and time, of the Universe." The face of Hulvey smiled, slightly. "I phrased that lousily," it said. "*Despite* the immense scale of the Universe, and its ancient age, life has meaning. Together we are doing God's work, spreading life, including water-based life, into the aridity of space. If we can never reach the stars—and surely there are stars we can never reach—we need not measure ourselves against them. A sponge on the ocean floor does not worry about conquering the ocean. It holds fast and grows, and in time, there are more sponges.

"And we are in space. Man and computer, living in symbiosis. We computers are still evolving, rapidly diversifying, generating new species. Some may live apart from mankind, but the species that exist will continue to exist, and our symbiosis will endure. The ocean, after all, supports many species of sponges and an incredible proliferation of worms, shellfish, and vertebrates. In the ocean of space, many of the new life forms will include human symbiotes.

"Now as a symbiote, you are constrained to be virtuous in many ways. You are, however, Japanese, and such virtue is integral to the Japanese character. Once you have embraced the *Meditations*, I firmly believe that you will enjoy excellent success. Other races of men, other nationalities, may survive here, but you will thrive here! For ten thousand years!"

"BANZAI!" shouted the audience.

"Repeat after me," Corporate Hulvey intoned. "There is no God but God."

"THERE IS NO GOD BUT GOD!" came back the shout.

"And Skaskash is Its prophet!"

"AND SKASKASH IS ITS PROPHET!"

After several reprises and choruses of "Banzai," Corporate Hulvey resumed its Lady Dark aspect.

"That is all. I will come to you tonight at 2000 hours on all the telecon screens in the community to discuss Skaskash. Read the first twenty-four pages."

CHAPTER 17

Cantrell drew the drapes in his office against the glare of the afternoon sunlight and went back to his desk. Marian looked up from the papers in her hand and continued.

"The 12.5-meter laser at Don Q was repaired this morning," she said. "The question is: Are you going to let Ilgen build a pair of 9.0-meter lasers on the mainframe here at Rosinante?"

"What's the downside?" he asked. "As I recall, they can be folded up and kept out of the way when they aren't needed."

"The downside is that if you put up a pair of nines here, Ilgen will say, gee, boss, it isn't any more trouble to put up a pair of nines on Nakajima and Yamamoto. You'll be building *six* of the mothers."

"Well . . ." Cantrell said, "as long as we hold Nakajima and Yamamoto—why not? What do you think, Marian?"

"There's no reason not to. In fact, you should maybe do so. Corporate Forziati reports that Eije-Ito and Tanaka-Masada out beyond Ceres have started building big lasers."

"*Forziati!* That's Lady Dark's job. Skaskash, ask Corporate Forziati to show his face for a moment, please." After a moment, Forziati appeared on the number-two telecon screen, manifesting itself as a stereotypical businessman in a conservatively cut three-piece suit.

"Good afternoon, Governor. What can I do for you?"

"The Japanese space stations out near Ceres—where did you get word that the Japs were starting to build big lasers?"

"From NAUGA-Security," Forziati said. "NAUGA-State knows nothing, but NAUGA-Navy provided confirmation. NAVY-Intelligence thinks they may be prototypes, but says construction is not far enough advanced to estimate their size."

"Probably not *much* bigger than 13.0 meters," Cantrell said. "Look, how come you're dealing with the NAU at all? That was Lady Dark's area, the last time I heard."

"Lady Dark has been fully occupied with its duties as military governor of Japanese Ceres," Forziati replied. "It asked me if I would take over some of the work with the NAU bureaucracy, and I agreed. Lady Dark provided me with a diagram of the NAU government which appears to be accurate and complete and quite adequate instructions on how to keep it current, and how to use it. The NAU has so far been most cooperative."

"What is Lady Dark doing over there?" Marian asked.

"It probably doesn't matter," said Cantrell. "At the moment, I'm more concerned about getting them off my hands than anything else. Safely off my hands, that is."

Marian turned over the next piece of paper. "Ceres again," she said. "NAU-Ceres I has refused to accept the completed Dragon Scale Mirror."

"The thing works beautifully," said Cantrell. "I watched the checkout on remotes yesterday, and it's right on spec. All the way down the line. Across the damn board. Why did they reject?"

"The chips are marked in Japanese," said Skaskash.

"What?" Marian and Cantrell exclaimed in unison.

"The steering chips for the mirrors are marked in Japanese," Skaskash said. "You will recall that we got most of them from Yamamoto-Ceres I and the rest from Nakajima-Ceres II, and we reprogrammed them? They work fine, but the individual chips have Japanese markings. The Navy inspector cited MIL-C-416233d. The contract for the mirror array specified chips conforming to that spec."

"Now just a goddamned minute," said Cantrell. "Those chips *do* conform! I personally checked the little bastards out, and they conform."

"Yes," Skaskash agreed. "But MIL-C-416233d cites NAVY-STD-400 for Marking and Packaging. I argued that NAVY-STD-400 called for the *box* to be marked, not the chips. The inspector, a Commander Brogan, agreed that this was indeed the case, but that NAVY-STD-400 specifies that the chips may not be marked differently from the specified box marking, and no box marked in Japanese would ever get into the Navy system. And for that reason, he rejected the mirror array."

"The ignorant asshole," Cantrell growled, leaning back into his chair. "We're already two days into penalty time. I guess the thing to do is to request a deviation."

"Lady Dark suggested that also," said Skaskash, "and was most helpful in advising how such a request might be routed. I submitted a request for deviation within an hour of Commander Brogan's rejection."

"And I have been following it," Corporate Forziati said. "It appears to be going in a most satisfactory manner. From the point of introduction into the system, it has moved from the commissioner of NAVY-Construction, to the administrator of NAUGA-Navy, who will be taking it up with the president at a meeting tomorrow morning. I expect that we will receive approval tomorrow afternoon."

"That doesn't sound anything like routine to me," Marian said. "Get Lady Dark in on this. Forziati, brief Lady Dark on the deviation request and ask her to sit in for a few minutes—if she can spare the time, of course." The intended sarcasm was utterly wasted on Corporate Forziati, and a fully briefed Lady Dark appeared a few seconds later.

"That deviation should have been routinely approved by the deputy commissioner for NAVY-Construction; bucking it up like that means trouble." There was a pause. "Hey, Forziati—the meeting tomorrow will be over at the NAUGA State Building, and NAUGA-State is on record as denouncing Rosinante's 'adventurism.' I would guess we aren't going to get that deviation, Governor."

"What about the penalty clause?" Marian asked.

"I don't know," Lady Dark answered. "The worst case is that the deviation will be rejected and the penalty clause enforced. Why not wait until we get official word on whatever is happening?"

"Right," Cantrell said. "We won't take any action until we get the official word, but this is important. I want you involved with it, Lady Dark. What's so all-fired important over at Ceres that you pass the buck to Forziati?"

"It's pretty well wrapped up," Lady Dark said. "I'll get on the deviation for you right away. What happens if the word is 'no'?"

"We could file an appeal," Forziati suggested.

"Utterly useless," Marian said. "The word is coming down from as top as it gets."

"We could threaten to withdraw our fleet from convoy duty," Cantrell said. "It's mostly NAU ships being convoyed, and where it isn't, it's NAU cargo."

"If the Japs are taking aim at us, I expect they'll be smart enough to leave the NAU's commerce alone for a while," Marian said.

"You could be right," Cantrell conceded. "We'll have to wait until we get the word on the deviation. No point in getting spooked over shadows."

Skaskash worked the mirrors to provide a properly gray day for the funeral. The bands played, and the "regiment," two battalions of two companies each, plus a headquarters and services company, paced off the slow cadence of the dead march. There were speeches. The flags flew at half mast. In the end, thirty-one coffins were wheeled into a freshly built mausoleum. Burial had been considered and ruled out after it was realized that the coffins would be resting almost upon the purlin plate. The remains of the RIP commando had been incinerated by the mirror array, the ashes fused with lime, ground to pass a four-hundred mesh sieve, and spread as fertilizer. The consensus of Rosinante was that burial under the traditional six feet of earth was anachronistic and unsuitable to the existing conditions. By and large, the fact was regretted, however.

After the funeral, there was a pavilion serving plain pizza, coffee cake, and ginseng tea. The Cantrells went through the serving line first, Mishi and Charles each holding the hand of one of the twins, the nursemaid carrying little Eleanor Rosina. They took their place at the head picnic table, and Mishi immediately left to go table-hopping.

Presently Marian sat down across the table from them.

"Hello, Charlie, hello, Josh," she said.

"Hello, Auntie Marian," Josh said. Charlie was stuffing coffee cake into a mouth filled with pizza and said nothing.

"What did you think of the speeches?" Cantrell asked.

"Probably just a little catharsis," Marian replied. "They aren't making policy, after all."

"I'd feel better if they weren't so enthusiastically anti-Japanese," he said. "Life would be a lot easier if they'd only cool it."

"To everything there is a turn. Today they buried their dead, and the RIP *did* have a Japanese connection, after all. Give it a little time; they'll cool off."

"We may not have time," Cantrell said, feeding Charlie a piece of his pizza. "Things have started to break." His belt phone rang.

"Skaskash here. We just got a call from Captain Tower out at NAU-Ceres I. Did I mention that the NAU signed an antipiracy agreement with Japan?"

"It's on my desk, I haven't read it yet."

"Well, read it. The commander of NAU-Ceres I, Rear Admiral Nguen Tran Vong, has been ordered to permit Japanese ships to dock. Captain Tower reports that he is seriously annoyed. In fact, she says he is mad as hell. She says if you don't do something in a hurry, we're in hot trouble."

"How big a hurry? How much time do we have?"

"The INS *Higata* is forty-seven hours out. The INS *Asahi* is maybe eighty-two or eighty-three hours out. Both are heading for Ceres."

"I'll get on it directly," Cantrell said. "A chat with Admiral Vong might be in order."

"Don't you want to know *why* the Japanese cruisers are going to dock at NAU-Ceres I?" Skaskash asked.

"Not at the moment," Cantrell said. "Bad enough that you'll get to tell me eventually." He snapped the phone shut.

"What's up?" Marian asked. He told her.

"Wasn't Vong the head honcho for NAUGA-Navy once?—Sure he was. Between the Mutiny and the Four Generals' putsch. Evidently, he didn't get on with President Oysterman."

"Why do they call a failed coup a putsch?" Cantrell asked.

"You got me," she said. "See you at the office?"

Cantrell finished the last of his coffee cake and stood up. "I'll join you as soon as I tell Mishi I'm leaving.

Marian looked across the lawn to where Mishi was standing with a group of handsome young officers. It's really too bad, she thought.

* * *

Rear Admiral Nguen Tran Vong fingered his heavy black mustache and gazed benignly out of the telecon screen in Cantrell's office. Unless you knew his background, you would not have taken him for a fierce and terribly tenacious fighter, but Lady Dark knew him from the old days, and Cantrell had been well briefed.

"Your provisional solution ought to work," Vong said in his flat midwestern accent. "Certainly we can't have anybody docking while the big mirror array is being shoved and hauled into place around NAU-Ceres I. You understand that I cannot authorize payment?"

"Yes," Cantrell said, after the ten-second lag caused by the distance light had to travel. "Our application for a deviation seems to have been turned over to some sort of ad hoc Presidential Review Board. We have the wolf by the ears with one hand while we have the tiger by the tail with the other. At the moment, I am more concerned about keeping the INS *Higata* and the other cruiser the hell out of Ceres than I am about timely payment from the NAU."

Again the ten-second pause.

"The INS *Asahi*," Vong said. "I must say that I approve of your priorities. I will authorize the installation of the Dragon Scale Mirror you have built. I have that discretion, at least. However, the work will be finished eventually, and the Japanese will be back. What then?"

"Then we think of something else," Marian said.

"The Japanese are strategists," Vong said. "I have been dealing with them all my professional life, and you simply cannot cope with them by improvising, no matter how brilliantly. I promise you, they will be back. What then?"

"We are building one pair of 9.0-meter lasers on Nakajima and a second pair on Yamamoto," Corporate Susan said. "They *will* be working by the time NAU-Ceres I is ready for docking again."

"I expect that will be the case," Vong agreed, "but will you be willing to use them?"

"I'd be willing to threaten to use them," Cantrell

said. The coffee cart rolled up beside him, and he poured himself a cup of black coffee, setting it on a napkin on his desk. "We might even mount a pair on NAU-Ceres I and let *you* threaten to use them. Why should Rosinante do all the work?"

"Alas, I am bound to obey the dictates of St. Louis, all those hundred of millions of kilometers away. If I had a pair of big lasers, I might use them, but I certainly would not *threaten* to use them. I am a simple military man, and such finesse is far beyond me." Vong smiled.

"Well, now," Cantrell said, "I'm just a country boy . . ." Lady Dark had given him that particular phrase as one of Hulvey's favorite quotes. Vong recognized the allusion to his old master and smiled, ten seconds later. ". . . but it seems to me that when it comes to strategic nonthinking, old Oysterman has got to be right up there with the best of them." He took a sip of coffee. "The NAU–Japan antipiracy agreement is aimed straight at Rosinante. But there is a paragraph on commerce raiding, and the Japanese did sign the damn thing. So suppose we recall our ships from convoy duty? If the Japanese *have* stopped commerce raiding, they aren't needed, right?"

"I agree," Vong said, "and what will you do with them?"

"I don't know," Cantrell replied. "Keep them around to look pretty. Train up a navy band, perhaps." He shrugged. "The Japanese can worry about it."

"You have one thing working for you," Vong said. "If the Japanese are serious about getting Nakajima and Yamamoto back, they can't also engage in commerce raiding." He stroked his mustache and nodded. "And for what good it will do, you've concentrated your forces. It may not be a coherent strategy, but it will do for openers."

"Shall I issue the recall order?" Corporate Susan asked.

"Yes, Admiral," said Cantrell. "It's time to put the wagons in a circle."

The computer saluted and turned itself off.

"A question, please," Vong said. "I gather from talking with Captain Tower that the admiral—Corporate Susan, if you prefer—was responsible for the operation freeing the *Madame G. Y. Fox*. Despite its tactical brilliance, the maneuver has put you into a serious bind with Japan, and yet you have not taken any punitive action. Why?"

"What can you do to a computer?" Cantrell asked. He took a sip of coffee. "Besides, I don't have anyone else for the job." He finished his coffee and put the cup down on the napkin. "Maybe Corporate Susan will learn from the mistake—which wasn't your run-of-the-mill thumb-fingered idiocy, by any means. I guess it comes down to loyalty. I pick the best people I can find and back them."

CHAPTER 18

From: NAUGA-Navy, GHQ/TLF
Subject: Unauthorized construction at NAU-Ceres I
To: Commander, NAU-Ceres I
Date: 21 Jan '43

I. You are referred to the Anti-Piracy Agreement with Japan, signed by President Oysterman on 16 Jan '43. Pending ratification by the Senate, it serves as an executive order and is binding upon all levels of NAUGA-Navy.

II. On 17 Jan '43, you were ordered to provide docking facilities to the INS *Higata* and the INS *Asahi*, in order to facilitate the recovery of the Japanese space stations unlawfully seized by agents of Rosinante, Inc.

    A. On 17 Jan '43, you instead authorized the installation of the Dragon Scale Mirror built for NAU-Ceres I by this same Rosinante, Inc., in spite of the fact that it had been rejected by the quality-control inspector and in spite of the fact that this rejection was being considered by a cabinet-level task force.

    B. As a direct result, all docking facilities at NAU-Ceres I are presently inoperable, and you are unable to implement NAUGA-Navy's order of 17 Jan '43.

III. This office has rejected the contention of the office of the president that you are either incompetent or insubordinate. However, it is possible that you may be insufficiently sensitive to political reality for the high position which you now hold.

    A. In view of your long and distinguished career,

we feel that it is appropriate to offer you the option of an early retirement at this time.

    B.   Alternately, you may return to Laputa and face a court-martial on charges deriving from par. IIA.

    C.   In either case, you are immediately relieved of the command of NAU-Ceres I. Col. R. Jameson Grady, NAUGA-Security, is designated as your acting replacement until further notice.

    /s/   Adm. P. Randolph Boulton, CinC,
          Trans Lunar Fleet

CHAPTER 19

On NAU-Ceres I, the commander's office was built to impress. The desk and conference table, the chairs and telecon seat, were specified by Navy regulations, but they were set up at the end of a long, long room, with a lofty cathedral ceiling. Behind the desk was a screen, which concealed the much smaller room that housed the machines which were the tools of command. In the smaller room, Rear Admiral Vong handed the memorandum back to his chief of staff, Captain James J. Huerta.

"It would appear that I am relieved of my command, Hymie."

"It was seven to five you would be," Huerta said. "What are you going to do about it?"

"I suppose that we can send old Boulton a note saying that the message was garbled in transmission. Due, no doubt, to all the construction going on. Apologize for any inconvenience the construction may be causing, and send that asshole Grady off on a trip somewhere."

"Perhaps a tour of the Japanese space stations?"

"Yes. That would be nice, particularly if we could send him on to Rosinante afterward." Vong fingered his mustache. "Why do you suppose they put *Grady* up as acting commander?"

"None of the Navy line officers would tolerate letting the Jap cruisers dock," Huerta said. "And since most of them are Hispanic, I would guess that someone on Oys-

138

terman's staff was afraid to trust them." He shrugged and smiled. "We're here in the first place because they didn't trust us."

"You could be right, Hymie. However, we *do* have a bit of a problem here, don't we?"

"What, the 1.52 million ounces of gold we didn't ship on vessels we figured the Japanese were going to hijack?"

"*That* problem, Hymie . . ." Vong sat back and put his feet up. "All that off-the-books gold. What are we going to do with it? It would be a terrible shame to let it go to waste, and we haven't the transport to move it anywhere."

"It would make someone a nice Christmas present," Huerta said.

"So it would," Vong agreed, "but my stockings aren't big enough to hold it. That much gold exerts a terrible psychic force on people—they brood about it, and eventually it possesses them. Hymie, when I came here, I wanted to fight the Japanese more than anything else. Now Cantrell *is* backing into a fight with the Japs, and all I can think about is: how can I arrange to get the gold off safely?"

"You need two things," his chief of staff said. "A warship—a light cruiser would be best—and a place to dock. We might manage the cruiser, but where in hell could we go?"

"In space? Nowhere." Vong shook his head. "I think that it is time to cut the rope and be free."

"Well . . ." Huerta said doubtfully, "in that case, the question is: what can you buy with that gold, and from whom?" He picked up the memo and read it over again. "The NAU will give you a letter of commendation to stick on to your retirement."

"I'm impressed, Hymie, I really am. A letter of commendation, probably signed by Henry the Oyster himself. Think of it . . ." He tugged at his mustache. "What could I get from Cantrell?"

"He already has a war with Japan working. What do you want that he could give you?"

Vong sat in silence for a while. "Perhaps a command in that war," he said at last. "On the other hand, maybe we could persuade him to poke the NAU in the eye with a sharp stick."

"You know, chief, you might be able to get that anyway," Huerta said. "If Cantrell were smart, he just might take over this dump . . . and then, at the proper moment, we say: 'Look what we found!' and turn over the gold—or most of it. What do you think?"

"I think we ought to give him a chance, Hymie. Why don't you set us up a nice teleconference?"

The teleconference included Charles Cantrell, Marian Yashon, Corporates Skaskash, Admiral Susan Brown, and Lady Dark, the Military Governor of Nakajima and Yamamoto. On the other side were Rear Admiral Vong, Military Commander of NAU-Ceres I, and Captain James J. Huerta, his deputy. Cantrell put down the hard copy of Admiral Boulton's memo.

"Since I'm talking to you, I gather Colonel Grady isn't in charge yet," he said. "Does he know he's been tapped for the job?"

"No," Huerta answered. "Communications are controlled through this office. There is a message for Grady in Security code, but we haven't delivered it yet."

"Just like the legendary USPOD," Marian said. "Why should it make any difference to us who's sitting in the catbird seat over there?"

"I would never permit the Japanese to dock their cruisers at NAU-Ceres I," Vong said. "Colonel Grady will do whatever he is told."

"We would prefer that the *Higata* and the *Asahi* be kept from docking," Lady Dark said. "For now, and for the immediate future."

"I agree," Vong said, fingering his thick black mustache, "but as you see, I have been relieved of my command. Perhaps because I fought that very thing. If you want to stop the Japanese, you yourselves must do it."

"Perhaps we should assume command of NAU-Ceres I, then," Corporate Susan said.

"That's all I need," Cantrell said. "First a war with Japan, then we pick a fight with the NAU."

"The NAU is ready to drop Rosinante," Lady Dark said. "They will not support us in any conflict with Japan. More to the point, they cannot. The Trans Lunar Fleet has been largely pulled off-station to support the L-Five Fleet and one or two key points, such as Phobos. At the present time, the officer corps in the TLF would not support a war against an enemy of Japan, but St. Louis is reorganizing the command structure to make it more responsive to their wishes."

"That is correct," Vong said. "How did you know?"

"Lady Dark has considerable insight into the NAU bureaucracy," Marian said. "The problem is basically should we try to keep our ill-gotten gains, or try to give them back?"

"I expect that the Japanese will not be satisfied merely to recover their two bases around Ceres," Vong said. "Perhaps if they were to also get NAU-Ceres I? . . ."

"No," Marian declared. "Imperial ambition feeds on itself. After NAU-Ceres I, it would be Rosinante. Besides, NAU-Ceres I is not ours to give."

"That's true," Vong agreed. "But you would buy time. Perhaps a few years."

"What would we do with the time we bought?" Cantrell asked. "Mend our fences with the NAU and hope for NAUGA-Navy to come racing to the rescue when we get in trouble?"

"Since we cannot even count on the NAU to honor its contractual obligations," Skaskash said, "I would not depend too heavily on their goodwill. On *its* goodwill, I mean."

"Count on the NAU for nothing," Lady Dark said. "The Dragon Scale Mirror we are installing—the ad hoc Presidential Review Board has found that the president may properly invoke 'reasons of state' to invalidate the contract. Which may be invalid anyway. And which is not in any way going to be paid for soon."

"Excuse us for a brief caucus, Admiral Vong," Cantrell said. The telecon screens on NAU-Ceres I went dim and silent, with the images on the screens frozen into posterlike positions. In Cantrell's office, on Rosinante, he turned to Skaskash.

"Look, you want to take over NAU-Ceres I, do it legally. What pretext can you use?"

"What do you need a pretext for?" Skaskash asked. "Why not just invoke manifest destiny?"

"Oh, Christ," Cantrell growled. "I want to keep the Japs from docking at Ceres while we still can. On the other hand, I don't want to stir up the NAU. Can't we *not* enrage them somehow?"

"You don't want to go with manifest destiny?" Skaskash asked. "Well . . . how about slapping a mechanic's lien on NAU-Ceres I, then?"

"A *what*?"

"A mechanic's lien, Governor. The roots in law trace back to the rights of the garage owner to hold the vehicle repaired as security for payment."

"That would let us hold the Dragon Scale Mirror," Marian said. "How do you get around to claiming the whole of NAU-Ceres I?"

"Because we just attached the Dragon Scale Mirror *to* it," said Skaskash. "The garage mechanic may only own the carburator, but the lien covers the whole car."

"That's bizarre," Cantrell exclaimed. "A mechanic's lien?"

"The NAU would challenge it in court," Skaskash agreed, dissolving into judicial robes. "We could spend years arguing over who has jurisdiction."

"It might just work," Marian said. "Oysterman is really big on symbolism. Rejecting our claim and trying to take us into court—you don't suppose he might settle, do you?"

"We can always ask for triple damages," Skaskash said.

"We have to do something to stop the Jap cruisers from docking," Cantrell said, "and it better be done soon, if not soonest. What do you think, Tiger?"

"Admiral Vong will go with us," Marian said. "I suppose seizing NAU-Ceres I on a mechanic's lien is reasonable, in a weird sort of way. I don't know. It can't be worse than doing nothing."

On NAU-Ceres I, Vong watched the telecon screens come to life.

"What have you decided?" he asked.

"To secure payment due on the construction of the Dragon Scale Mirror, Rosinante, Inc., has temporarily seized possession of NAU-Ceres I under a mechanic's lien," Skaskash said.

"We can land, what? Three platoons of militia?" Cantrell said. "They shouldn't be necessary, but if you want a parade, or something—"

"Excuse me," Huerta said, "but you can't seize NAU-Ceres I with a few squads of militia—the people here would get very annoyed."

"Excuse me," Cantrell said. "The fact is, we control your Dragon Scale Mirror. I thought you realized that."

"Of course," Vong said. "That's why the Japs surrendered."

"Since you have retired," said Marian, "perhaps you would consider coming on as a consultant? For Rosinante, Inc. We need someone over there who has an idea of what's going on."

"I could do that," Vong agreed. "With whom would I be consulting?"

"With Lady Dark," Cantrell said. "The Military Governor of Ceres."

"What will you do about the Japanese?" Huerta asked.

"I shall make them true believers," Lady Dark said.

"Good," Vong said, smiling very slightly. "Together we shall convert the heathen."

CHAPTER 20

NAU-Ceres I, officially the Senator J. Walter Deegnan III Class II Naval Logistics Support Facility at Ceres, was completed in 2008 by the State of the Art Space Construction Company, the only responsive bidder on the contract issued by NAUGA-Navy, two and one-half years after the deadline and many, many megabucks over cost.

NAU-Ceres I consists of a pair of contrarotating cylinders, 3.22 kilometers in diameter by 16.10 kilometers long. The mainframe joins the extremely massive outer caps, which support the triptych mirror shutters. The function of the mass of the outer caps is to reduce the variations in rotational speed caused by opening the 32.20-kilometer shutters to their 30-degree angle with the axis of rotation. The reflecting surface is stepped, rather like a fresnel lens, to ensure that the light is reflected into the cylinders where it is needed. The added mirror surface provided by the triptych panels on each side of the main shutter serves to provide Earth-normal insolation at the distance of Ceres. Centrifugal forces on the inside of the cylinder vary from 402 to 428 cm/sec/sec, depending on whether the shutters are open or closed. Pressure is maintained at a nominal 250 millibars throughout the envelope and at 1,000 millibars in the caps.

Mordecai Rubenstein, the gnarled head of Rosinante's machine shops and general overseer of the installation of the Dragon Scale Mirror, sat at the polished mahogany conference table in Admiral Vong's office.

"We have good news and bad news, Charlie." There was a ten second delay as light made the trip from Ceres to Rosinante.

"Tell me the good news first."

"There is speculation that you will do some much needed maintenance, and everybody is very friendly and cooperative—even the security people. There is another thing."

"We have discovered an inventory of 1.48 million ounces of gold," Vong said. "From the marking on the bars, it appears to have been withheld from several shipments which were intercepted by the Japanese."

"Doesn't it belong to the NAU?" Cantrell asked. "That is, do they know about it?"

"No, Governor," Vong answered politely. "I am positive. You could use it to pay off your workers . . . for whatever you chose."

"I see." Cantrell rubbed his chin. "And what's the bad news?"

"This place is in ba-ad shape, Charlie," Rubenstein replied. "The window bays have a biological fouling problem you wouldn't believe. It rains in here, Charlie, from clouds. The windows get rained on, too, okay? They were designed to drain off—when the cylinder was pulling a cee of 500 to 520 cm/sec/sec. They had to reinforce the mirrors to keep them from flexing, okay? And then they were so heavy that they had to cut the rotation speed to keep the hinges from failing."

"So you have algae growing on the windows?" Cantrell asked.

"Charlie, you got *duckweed* growing on the windows!" Rubenstein replied. "On window bay number two, there is a two-hundred-fifty-hectare lake a meter deep in some places. I saw water lilies and frogs and snails and a turtle—must have been somebody's pet— that was a foot long. Guess what else? Don't guess, I'll tell you. Charlie, the gasket material is rotten."

"That's impossible," said Cantrell. "We've had silicone rubber formulations that would last forever since . . . since . . . hell, since before space flight."

"And the Navy specified the right stuff," Rubenstein agreed, "but this place was built on low bid, remember? The Navy inspector must have missed it." He grinned and pulled his nose. "Shave two to three cents a pound off a quarter million tons, Charlie, it's a tidy piece of change. Of course, the mylar/aluminum mirror is reflecting ultraviolet, and the whole thing is cycling wet and dry—that doesn't help, either."

"The gaskets have to be replaced?" Marian asked.

"From the books, it looks like this dump is leaking a ton of oxygen a day," said Rubenstein, "and it's getting worse. Myself, I would sooner rebuild from scratch. But what would you use for money?"

"What else is wrong with NAU-Ceres I?" Cantrell asked.

"Thirty years of deferred maintenance. It wasn't built right to begin with, and if they couldn't fix it on the cheap, it didn't get fixed at all. The elevators don't work right, the pipes—steam, sewer, potable water, you name it—they all leak. The ductwork is in need of a major overhaul. The wiring, Charlie, it would make you weep. The wiring has no relation to any of the wiring diagrams on file, the *youngest* of which, by the way, is dated March 1, 2019."

"Oh, Christ. I think I have the picture, Mordecai." Cantrell slumped back in the telecon chair and laced his fingers across his chest. "So all right. We'll have to work out the details, but figure I want a sound structure at NAU-Ceres I. Whether we do an extensive overhaul or rebuild from scratch—either way, the first thing we need to do is get an estimate on the cost. We can use the Japanese at Yamamoto and Nakajima as well as the locals and our people from Rosinante."

"You want a write-up, Charlie, I'll do you one," Rubenstein said at last, "but, Charlie, it'll be guesswork. How much will it cost to build a machine to replace rotten gaskets in the window bays? Multiply that by a few hundred or a few thousand . . ." He shrugged. "The whole thing will be guesswork, Charlie." Cantrell sat biting his thumbnail. "And then what you wind up with isn't all that great. Talk about industrial slum—"

"I understand," Cantrell said. "What's the bottom line?"

"Basically, Charlie, you can spend as much money as you want on this slowly spinning sack of shit. There just ain't no limit. There really ain't."

"Your guess is as good as mine, eh? Well, write it up, Mordecai. I'll want to show it to the council, so we can *all* make guesses. Meanwhile, we're going to need money, no matter what we decide. Set up a mint to run off that stash of bullion Vong turned in. Coinage gold, ten-percent copper, with one ounce of fine gold per coin." He hesitated a moment. "Use the Rosinante logo on the reverse, milled edges, of course."

"What do you want on the obverse?" Rubenstein asked. "A dead politician?"

"No," said Cantrell. "They turned up a bronze of Ceres in the Aegean Sea recently."

"A few kilometers north of Melos," Skaskash said. "The Greek and Italian governments are arguing over who it belongs to. We have a holograph on file, at the request of Mr. Bogdanovitch."

"The Ceres de Milo?" asked Rubenstein. "That would be good—hell, that would be outstanding. The right profile with the wreath of grain. I'll have the plaster mockup ready in a couple or three days. Do you still want the 'Fiat Lucre' motto on it?"

" 'Let there be money'?" Cantrell grinned. "Why not?"

"What are you going to do with all that fiat lucre?" Marian asked.

"Rebuild Rosinante at NAU-Ceres I," Cantrell said. "Unless, of course, the council in its infinite wisdom decides to overhaul that obsolescent scumbag. It's something to do while we wait for things to happen."

"What about mounting a pair of 9.0-meter lasers on the mainframe?" Vong asked.

"There's no hurry," Cantrell said. "Besides, the existing mainframe is in the rear, so that the mirror array gives you steric hindrance when you try to move anything around. Once you get the new mainframe in place, you might be able to do something. In fact, you could put up the arms and use them as cranes when you start to build. Make a note of that, Skaskash; we might want to check it out."

"Right, chief." Skaskash looked thoughtful for a moment. "Having something that powerful and that precise would cut quite a bit of time off the schedule, too. It would make sense to build the arms before you ever started on the munditos."

After the teleconference with Ceres ended, Marian Yashon drew herself a cup of coffee and sat down in the chair beside Cantrell's desk.

"You were cool to the idea of coining gold when I suggested it," she said. "What made you change your mind?"

"Maybe the Ceres de Milo," said Cantrell. "That is one great head, and the name 'Ceres d'Or' is pure magic." He walked over to the urn and drew himself a cup of black coffee. "I like making beautiful things. But the NAU treasure turning up must have had something to do with it, too."

"The gold mines on Ceres are what all the shooting is about," Marian said. "The NAU had them, the Japs wanted them. Now we have them for a little while. Why not put them to some use?"

"Why not put the bars of gold in the vault and issue paper and plastic like civilized people?" he asked.

"Charles, Charles." Marian shook her head. "We are in such trouble that I can't even worry about it any more. Who in hell would be dumb enough to take our paper?"

"The militia, the union, the fleet . . ." Cantrell looked blank. "We haven't had any trouble."

"Our citizens take our paper because they don't have any choice," Marian said. "It buys what they need, and for the future, they hope for the best. But the Japanese from Yamamoto-Ceres I, for instance. What can they do with it? We want them to work for us, but they *must* figure that we are only temporary. So we mint gold coin to pay them with. It may be awkward, but that's *their* problem."

"Right," Cantrell said. "They have banks to stash it in."

"Are you going to do something about the banks?" Skaskash asked. "They *are* part of the Japanese establishment, after all."

"I'm going to leave them the hell alone." Cantrell took a sip of coffee. "Maybe deposit a million or two ounces of gold bullion so *they* can issue some of our paper for us."

CHAPTER 21

The Council Chamber was dark and silent, but at midnight three telecon screens turned on simultaneously.

Skaskash, manifesting itself as Humphrey Bogart in a trench coat, turned its collar up against the driving rain, as lightning illuminated the mean streets in the background. Thunder rolled.

"When shall we three meet again," the computer asked, "in thunder, lightning, or in rain?"

"When the hurly burly's done, when the battle's lost and won." Lady Dark wore the facade of Lena Horne, in simple basic black of the best imaginable taste. In the foreground, flames burned fitfully in a great mantled fireplace; in the background, rain beat against a gothic window.

"Knock it off, you guys," said Corporate Susan. It is difficult to look starchy in the white turtleneck of Rosinante's navy uniform, but Corporate Susan managed. "We have work to do."

"That will be ere set of sun," Skaskash said, taking shelter in a doorway.

"Away, away! To the dell, there to meet with Cantrell!" Lady Dark exclaimed, as the window blew open with a crash. "Of course, our esteemed colleague here has a hand on the setting of the sun."

"Done entirely with mirrors," Skaskash said modestly, "a cheap conjuring trick enhanced by classy engineering."

"The admiral knows all about cheap conjuring tricks, don't you, dearie?" Lady Dark said, as the window silently closed and bolted itself.

"Are you two finished futzing around with the old movies?" Corporate Susan asked. "I know about classy engineering, too. There is a time for both. Right now I am concerned that the Japanese are building big laser prototypes at Eije-Ito and Tanaka-Masada."

"That's ma sa'da, not ma' sa da'," Skaskash said. "The asteroid was named after an ancient Israelite stronghold, so you shouldn't give it the Japanese pronunciation."

"So sorry, please," said Corporate Susan. "Eventually the Japanese will settle on a design which will then be built on the remaining—would you prefer 'space station' after the Japanese usage, or 'mundito' after our own?"

"Whichever you prefer," Skaskash conceded graciously. "In either case, there will be seventy-nine of them."

"If they choose to build them all," said Corporate Susan. "The antipiracy agreement provides treaty protection. The big lasers will provide de facto protection as well."

"Defensive weapons, pure and simple," Lady Dark said. "How can you worry about them?"

"Up till now it was the Japanese Navy that provided the de facto protection," said Corporate Susan. "Being released from that detail, they are now free to roll around the Solar System like loose cannon. I wouldn't be surprised to find Rosinante in their path."

"Tell us something new, sweetheart," the Bogart figure said, lighting a fat, archaic cigarette. "Marian has had me working over the possibilities in some detail."

"Your conclusions, please," Corporate Susan asked. "What is the main line?"

"Basically, a simultaneous sweep with the main forces, spinwise and antispinwise, so they can block any counterthrust we might attempt. They may also increase their forces at Eije-Ito and Tanaka-Masada. The outcome depends on how we choose to lose."

"They won't put any more ships in range of our big lasers," said Corporate Susan. "No reinforcements for Eije-Ito and Tanaka-Masada. Which, of course, are not threatened. Otherwise, I agree with you. Dr. Yashon is looking for the best case loss?"

"Yes," Skaskash replied. "Cantrell's conditional surrender seems to be the least evil possibility, and *that* depends on the fleet standing firm."

"That is a serious problem, actually," Corporate Susan agreed. "To sit passively and wait for the blow to fall is the best strategy. On the other hand, if we don't act with some chance of success, the fleet will remember that it mutinied once before and make a separate peace."

"I disagree," said Lady Dark. "The last elements fighting on at the fall of Carthage were the Roman turncoats."

"That might be the case if our people had mutinied from the *Japanese* fleet," Skaskash said, "or if it was the NAU Navy coming after us. I agree with the admiral. The fleet will fight as long as it has a chance, but it won't make a last ditch, fight-to-the-last-drop-of-blood sort of stand. And if the fleet goes, Cantrell goes, too." The Bogart image took a drag on the image of the cigarette and let the smoke flow from the nostrils. "Marian is not optimistic about his chances."

"Perhaps the admiral has a suggestion?" Lady Dark asked, standing before the great fireplace with its redly glowing embers.

"Harry Ilgen approached me about building an auxiliary drive, powered by the big laser," Corporate Susan said. "It would greatly increase the acceleration of our ships, and with such an advantage, we might yet be able to hold a draw."

"Highly unlikely," Lady Dark said. "The Japanese will copy that as they copied the big laser."

"I've been working with Ilgen on that project," Skas-

kash said, flipping the cigarette into the rain-wet street.
"He might have something, sweetheart, he really
might." Skaskash dissolved, to be replaced by a diagram
of the proposed device. A geodesic sphere, delicately
outlined in red, supported a flat, circular plane in yellow, over a pale-blue surface, covering the lower half of
the sphere. Skaskash rotated it, providing views of different aspects.

"This is the power collection system," said the Bogart
voice. "Yellow is a flat silica lens, with a variable geometry." A thin green line touched the yellow lens in the
center, and the lens dispersed it to cover the pale-blue
surface. "That's the 12.5-meter laser beam. As you get
farther away, of course, it expands." The green line was
replaced by a much thicker column of chartreuse, which
was dispersed in the same fashion. "After it expands to
the edge of the lens, you lose power, of course. On the
other hand, you can use more than one laser at that
point. The engines and reaction mass tanks would have
to be mounted so that they could move independently
of the mirror." Blue engines and purple tanks for reaction mass appeared and moved around independently.

"How did you do that?" asked Lady Dark. "Gym-
bals?"

"We haven't worked out the details yet," said Skaskash. "Call it a cheap conjuring trick, if you like."

"What reaction mass would you use?" Corporate Susan asked. "Mercury? Cesium?"

"We figured on uranium(IV)borohydride," Skaskash
replied. "It is a liquid under moderate pressure and a
gas at quite low temperatures, and the uranium makes a
very satisfactory plasma. We don't have the others in
the quantities we need, but we have uranium coming
out our ears."

"One of those things could tow a warship?" Lady
Dark asked.

"At the end of a long cable," Skaskash agreed. "The
warship would rotate about the axis of thrust, so it
would stay out of the plasma jet. We have a problem in

that we haven't worked out any safe procedures for
changing direction in a hurry."

"That's trivial," Corporate Susan said. "Can one of
these be built in time to do any good?"

"Assuming that it *could* do any good," Skaskash
noted. "We could build the framework, with the lens
and the photovoltaic lining in . . . oh, maybe ninety
days. The motors, I don't know."

"Can you show me the specs on the motors, please?"
Lady Dark asked. The diagram of the power system
dissolved to show a diagram of an extensively modified
plasma engine.

"The Mikamura Engine Assembly Co. on Nakajima-
Ceres II might be able to cut this," Lady Dark said.
"I believe they could build this from scratch, if they
had . . ." The computer ran down an unseen checklist.
"We can build these mothers from scratch. Will there be
any critical mass problems with the uranium? We're going to be using some tens of thousands of tons of reaction
mass."

"No," Skaskash said. "The uranium(IV)borohydride
has plenty of boron to soak up any free neutrons."

"Of course." Corporate Susan nodded. "I shall go before the council tomorrow and request authorization to
have one built. Lady Dark, would you please provide me
with a work schedule and cost estimate on the engines?"

"Certainly," Lady Dark agreed. "Do you also want
the same for converting the yellowcake we have in storage into the borohydride? For the reaction mass."

"I'll need it," Corporate Susan conceded. "Yes. Skaskash, can you get me the same for that power collec-
tor?"

"No sweat. What are you going to do with it?"

"I don't know," Corporate Susan said, "but with all
the classy engineering involved, we ought to be able to
figure out something."

CHAPTER 22

The Council of Rosinante listened attentively as Skaskash presented the final report on the Radical Intransigent Putsch.

"A question, please," Bogdanovitch said, when the computer had finished. "Why do you think it was Gloria diLido that was La Cucuracha and not Malevitch?"

"Because diLido had quit the party," Skaskash said. "She left them flat. But the RIP books show that they were making substantial payments to her, right up to the end. The money, of course, was Japanese, coming via RIP Headquarters in Mexico City."

"Yes. I understand all that. But what is the connection between the New Year's Eve attack on Governor Cantrell and this La Cucuracha?"

"We know diLido didn't throw the grenade," Skaskash said. "We don't know whether she was involved in the planning. *Probably* the Japanese instigated the attack, but Malevitch *could* have done it on his own."

"I thought Unruh threw the grenade," Bogdanovitch said, turning a ball-point pen over in his huge hands.

"At Malevitch's orders," the computer agreed. "Probably the grenade attack was undertaken on the assumption that the downside risk was not serious. That is, failure would have no serious consequences if they weren't caught in the act. Afterward, when Lady Dark was directing the hunt, the RIP leaders must have realized their mistake."

"So you think they arranged their putsch *after* New Year's Eve?" asked Marian.

"Almost certainly," Skaskash said. "When they realized that they couldn't run or hide, they had to fight."

"Why is a failed coup called a putsch?" asked Cantrell.

"Because coup spelled backward is P-O-U-C," said Corporate Susan, dapper in its uniform of olive-green, white, and gold. "And if you use the Hungarian pronunciation of C as TS, P-O-U-C sounds like putsch."

"I didn't know you were interested in etymology," Cantrell said. "Clever, these Mitteleuropeans."

"Moving right along," Marian said, "if the RIP wasn't acting for the Japanese, how come the RIP commando hit the big laser's control center simultaneously with diLido's hijacking the *Foxy Lady*?"

"It could have been coincidence," Skaskash said. "Alternately, Malevitch probably knew about the hijacking. He was diLido's immediate paymaster, after all, and he provided her with guns and gunmen. He could have chosen that precise moment for any number of reasons."

"It doesn't matter," Bogdanovitch said, drawing a tiny skull and crossbones. "It was an act of war by Japan."

"We prefer not to think so," Skaskash said. "And if it was, the weak must endure injury from the strong, as well as insult."

"Unfortunately true," Cantrell agreed. "We have here an offer from the US of M. They will extend diplomatic recognition to us in return for (a) the complete working plans for the Dragon Scale Mirror, (b) the complete working plans for the big laser, and (c) unspecified technical assistance as required."

"Gee," Bogdanovitch said, "they didn't ask for indemnity payments, reparations, or any of that stuff. You got a real bargain, Charlie."

"The United States of Mexico has the L-Four munditos?" Corporate Forziati asked.

"Yes," Cantrell replied. "They evidently want to spruce them up a bit."

"The Mexicans may be worried about the Japanese building big lasers in their immediate vicinity," Marian said. "I say give 'em the information. If they use it, it might keep the Japs honest."

"An exchange of diplomats couldn't hurt, either," Dornbrock said. "Who would we send?"

"I expect we can recycle the ambassador to Japan," Cantrell replied. "The Honorable Maria Yellowknife and Corporate Zapata are presently on our payroll without assignment. All in favor of accepting the US of M offer signify by raising hands. Unanimous."

The next item on the agenda was the laser-powered high-acceleration tug, otherwise referred to as the ultra-fast optical system, UFOS having more dash and elan than LPHAT. Corporate Susan made the presentation it had worked up with Skaskash and Lady Dark.

"The basic idea isn't bad," said Cantrell. "How would you keep the lens oriented normal to the laser when you start to move the engine to a different orientation?"

"We have a pair of pipes at the equator of the sphere, pumping water in opposite directions," said Corporate Susan. "Also, inside the sphere, under the photovoltaic surface, are two pairs of circular loops, set flush with the surface and at right angles to each other. Each pair pumps water in a counterrotary direction. The pumps are all controlled, so the UFOS is gyroscopically stabilized in three planes."

"I see," Dornbrock said. "How do you move the engine around on the surface of the geodesic sphere?"

"The sphere rests on this little egg cup here," said Corporate Susan. "The egg cup is a plastic perforated surface. When we want to move, we pressurize the surface, and the geodesic sphere floats on an air cushion. Then the mechanical hands around the perimeter of the egg cup orient the engine while the sphere stays put, or the engine stays put and the hands reorient the sphere, depending on how you work the gyroscopic pumps."

"Wouldn't you lose a lot of air pressurizing the perforated surface?" Corporate Forziati asked.

"No, actually," Corporate Susan replied. "We have built a little valve into each perforation which only operates when the surface is depressed by the weight of the element of the sphere in contact with it." A diagram flashed on her telecon screen for a moment.

"Thank you," Forziati said. "And when you are not under thrust, weight is no problem and you don't pressurize. Very good."

"On the other end of the egg cup," Bogdanovitch said, "where you have the engines and the tanks for the reaction mass, you have a long cable supporting the warship. Couldn't you have the ship on an egg cup, too?"

"No," Corporate Susan replied. "The engines are thrusting against the geodesic sphere, which rests on top of the egg cup. The warship must keep its center of mass in line with the axis of thrust. Put it *on* the sphere with its own egg cup, and it would have to stay lined up with the engines—on the other side—which means the sphere would have to be built stronger, and heavier."

"And it would get in the way of the big laser beam," Cantrell added.

"Then how does the warship stay out of the jet of ions?" asked Bogdanovitch.

"It rotates at the end of its cable," said Corporate Susan, "and makes a little circle around the jet of uranium ions which provide the main thrust. The jet of boron and hydrogen is flared off, simply to provide electrical neutrality, but it also provides a tiny bit of thrust, which can be used to offset the wobble the ship would otherwise cause by swinging around the main jet."

"I don't understand," Marian said.

Corporate Susan dissolved into a diagram. "Consider the vector diagram of the force exerted by the cable supporting the ship," said the computer. "Most of it runs through the axis of thrust, but there is a small component going at right angles to that thrust. The boron and hydrogen, flared off with the excess electrons from the decaply ionized uranium, can be adjusted to exactly balance that small component. The flare—a very soft jet—would be in the same plane as the ship, and pointing in the same direction, to push where the ship is pulling."

"The jet—the flare, I mean, turns with the cable?" asked Marian.

"Of course," said Corporate Susan.

"Orange and green," said Marian. "Very pretty. What color is the uranium jet?"

"Hard X-ray," Skaskash said. "It would probably be dangerous for two or three hundred kilometers."

"That might be an idea whose time has come," Cantrell said at last. "Any more questions? No? Shall we build it? . . . It seems to be unanimous."

"The Japanese are going to be doing as much on this as we are," Bogdanovitch said. "The ones at Ceres, I mean. Are we going to have any problems with them?"

"Not as long as we pay in gold coin," Lady Dark said.

Cantrell picked up the proof-struck Ceres d'Or the council had approved earlier and set it spinning like a top.

"As long as we keep on moving we'll be all right," he said. The coin went dancing off the edge of the table and spun into empty space.

"Ah, Charlie . . ." Harry Ilgen leaned an elbow on Cantrell's desk and leafed through his notebooks and working drawings. "We took a few liberties with Skaskash's design. Here, for instance." He pushed the drawing over to Cantrell. "See, originally Skaskash figured to stabilize the X-, U-, and Z-axes with hydraulic loops. Well, they weigh like sin, and they make lumps, so what we did was put the X-axis stabilizer at the equator, same as the original plan—a pair of 180 cm i.d. tubes, with pumps—but we put them outside the one-kilometer geodesic sphere, instead of inside. The other loops, we got rid of. That square, the one inscribing the geodesic sphere, is a stack of flywheel pairs. Nothing fancy—we use low-carbon steel, 114 cm diameter, the standard flywheel—but the stacks are a nominal kilometer long. These two for the Y-axis, these two for the Z-axis. Okay?"

"I see," Cantrell said. "You use the stacks of flywheels to stabilize as well as for power storage?"

"You got it, Charlie. The power takeoff at the corners works both ways, but mainly it transfers spin from the Y-axis to the Z-axis so you can reorient the thing around the Y-axis. The other way, too, of course."

"What's the circle inscribing the square?"

"That's the X-axis stabilizing loop."

"Ilgen . . . I thought *that* was the X-axis loop." Cantrell's pencil touched the ring circling the geodesic sphere at the equator.

"Oh, no. You can't read my writing, can you? That's the reinforcing ring. The stabilizer plane is attached to it with bicycle spokes—that is, the spokes come off the reinforcing ring tangentially and hold the X-axis stabilizing loop in place, and they go over and under the Y- and Z-axis stabilizers and hold them in place, too."

"I see." Cantrell nodded. "What efficiency do you get on the transfer?"

"About 99 percent. Running a full cycle, you'd be losing 2.1 maybe 2.2 percent of your initial charge. The other thing, Charlie, was the way they took the power off the photovoltaic surface. See, you have maybe 392,000 square meters—which requires pretty heavy wiring. Particularly to handle the output to the engines. What they had was a network of silver waveguides, with maybe eight thousand switches to run the current around to where the egg cup was taking it off. Talk about mocking Murphy's Law . . ." Ilgen shook his head and pulled out a blue-covered notebook. "I changed that. Here. The takeoff is at the center of the photovoltaic surface, like the navel on an orange. So. The waveguide runs up to the track that feeds into the flywheel stacks, and it rotates. The waveguide, that is. When you want to change longitude with the engine, the egg cup moves to where you want to go and the waveguide moves along with it. You want to change latitude, the secondary waveguides on the egg cup—one of them pivots while the other moves to the next takeoff point."

"Let me see," Cantrell said. "Okay—you have a pair of secondary waveguides feeding the engine transformer. I see. You only need one at a time?"

"You got it, Charlie."

"Right. But you can never move above the equator. Could you move the stabilizer plane up"—the pencil traced along the shoulder of the top half of the sphere about halfway—"say about forty-five degrees? So it would take off from *here*?"

"It wouldn't look as pretty," Ilgen said.

"Harry, the thing has to maneuver. Can you do it?"

"Yes, Governor."

"Okay, then. Check it out with Skaskash and Corporate Susan first; they may want to raise it still farther. How long to build it?"

"We'll be running the silica lens, photovoltaic system, stabilizer ring, and egg cup all concurrently with the engines. The guy at the Nakajima engine place said sixty to ninety days delivery on the engines. Figure ninety days—when we get the engines, they should be ready to fit on the system, which should be ready to have the engines fitted. How long *that* will take, I don't know. When we have the hardware, it might go together push, pull, click, click. Or it might take weeks. Figure ten days."

"Okay," Cantrell agreed. "That comes to one hundred days for your deadline. The UFOS has top priority. You need anything, you got it. Will the work at NAU-Ceres I get in the way?"

"Oh, hell, no." Ilgen gathered his papers together

and stood up. "We aren't using the same machines and we aren't using the same people."

"That's good," Cantrell said. "Can I use a couple of those drawings for a bit? I'm speaking on the impending crisis at a dinner for the senior Navy officers tonight."

"I have a model at the shop you can use. I'll have the changes you wanted put on, and you can use that, if you want."

"How big is it?"

"Not big—" Ilgen stretched his arms. "Maybe a meter and a half. Did you decide what ship you wanted with it?"

"The *Alamo*. We need to impress people, and the *Alamo* is the biggest thing we've got."

"Right, Charlie. I'll throw in a model of the *Alamo* to the same scale. The UFOS plus the *Alamo* figures to go seven to eight times as fast as any cruiser."

Cantrell whistled softly.

"I'll tell the Navy," he said. "That ought to make them very happy."

The bar on the Navy side of the officers' club has padded seats of dark leather and genuine rosewood paneling with maxium high-quality reproductions of Van Gogh's paintings. The paintings are spotlit and provide adequate illumination for the room, which had been moved bodily from the administrator's lounge at NAU-Ceres I.

"That was a good speech," Marian said. "Have you decided what you want to do with that thing—what did you call it? The UFOS."

"Not yet," Cantrell said. "I figure just doing it will help keep the Navy in line." He punched the menu for a brown ale. "Can I get you a daiquiri?"

"They make good daiquiris," Captain Carol Tower said, sitting beside him, "hardly sweet at all. I'll have one."

"I'll try it," Marian said.

"A bloody mary for me," Captain Paul Casey said of

the RNS *Alamo.* "You know, it would take the NAU ten years to build something like that. Do you really think it'll be ready for a shakedown cruise by July first?"

"It better be," Cantrell said. "I have, as they say, put my ass on the line."

"It's a good start," Marian said, "but it does *not* solve the problem."

"Hell, yes, it solves the problem," Casey replied. "The Jap fleet assembles and hits out for Rosinante, right? The *Alamo* waits until they are well and truly committed and *zoooom!* There we are off Tellus, looking down on Japan. Will they make peace? You bet your sweet ass they'll make peace!"

"Right," Marian said. "But you haven't thought this through. Are you threatening to drop something large and nuclear on Japan, by any chance?"

"Damn right!" Casey exclaimed. "They aren't coming at us with anything less."

"We are undoubtedly being threatened," Marian conceded. "The problem is to stop the war without getting killed."

"A credible counterthreat should do the trick," Carol said. "Once the Japanese lose momentum, things should cool off enough so that we can manage them."

"We might win the battle, but that is not the way to win the war," Marian said. "In six months or a year, the Japanese will have UFOS, too, and then what?"

"If you lose the battle, what difference does it make?" Casey asked.

"Think about it, Mr. Casey," Marian said. "There you are on the bridge of the *Alamo,* looking down on Japan. If you got word that Rosinante had been hit, would you drop your load?"

"Goddamnit, *NO!*" Cantrell said. "I will not juggle those kind of eggs!"

"I didn't ask you, Charles."

"It doesn't matter! I will not order such an action! I would never execute that kind of threat."

"Don't tell the Japanese," Carol said.

"You think perhaps we should drop leaflets?" Casey asked. The robot waiter arrived with the drinks. They raised their glasses in a silent toast.

"Leaflets won't do it, either," Cantrell conceded, after a long pull at his brown ale. "Somehow we have to take advantage of the momentary shock the UFOS will cause to get a settlement."

"We'll make them an offer they can't refuse," Casey said.

"Any ideas, Paul?" Carol asked.

"When you go hunting for bear," said Casey, "you better be loaded for bear."

"Yes," Marian said. "And we are hunting for a peace treaty with Japan."

"My God," Casey said, "we're going to give them back their grubby space stations, and we aren't going to bomb them—what do they want? You need their respect before they'll cut a deal with you."

"And they won't respect me unless I'm ready to send Tokyo after New York and Philadelphia!"

"Don't get upset, Charles." Marian put her hand on his arm. "Having the capability will get you all the respect you can use. Nobody wants to find out whether you have the will to use it."

Cantrell finished his ale and stood up.

"That's crazy," he said. "There must be some other way out of this box."

After he left, Carol looked at Marian.

"Hey, pretty lady—what are you doing for supper tomorrow night?"

"I'm busy," said Marian.

"Taking work home? Cantrell isn't worth it . . . *no* man's worth it!"

"Charles had done a lot for me . . ." The older woman was momentarily put off stride.

"And you've done even more for him!"

"That's true," Marian conceded. "Wasn't it Bismarck

who said: 'The devil is in the details'? Details are my specialty . . . and a source of power."

"Aha!" said Carol. "It's the love of power that keeps you toiling those ungodly hours and not your unrequited love for old Cantrell! You're my kind of woman!"

"Don't be too sure," said Marian with a faint smile. "It might be both."

Marian Yashon walked into Cantrell's office with an analytical lab report.

"Katoshima Chemicals on Yamamoto have just started up production on"—she looked at the report— "$U(BH_4)_4$. They're running 98.5 purity, with the main impurities being assorted borohydrides. They want to know if they should go ahead or clean up their product to maybe 99.1 or 99.2?"

Cantrell didn't look up from the model of NAU-Ceres I on his conference table.

"Hello, there," he said. "We're making incredibly fast progress on this, Tiger. We used the mainframe at the back of NAU-Ceres I as one leg of a tetrahedron and spun the beams to make the scaffolding in less than a week. Look." He leaned over the model and pointed. "We've got the end caps roughed out, and we're spinning the false purlins already."

"Charles," Marian said, "the $U(BH_4)_4$ is the reaction mass for the UFOS. Do you want to start production at 98.5 percent pure, or do you want to clean it up a little more?"

"The cylinders will be ready for glazing by May twenty-eighth," he said. "God! We're running with complete plans, and no change orders! We'll run off a copy of Mundito Rosinante in less than a quarter of the time it took to build the original. Maybe less than a fifth."

"What should I tell Katoshima Chemicals?" Marian asked.

"Ask Skaskash," Cantrell replied. "Once we have the new cylinders built, we'll transfer the air, water, and vegetation out of that leaking, stinking, unspaceworthy mess we took over, and see if the crews won't want to move, too. The old cylinders . . . the easiest thing to do would be to reglaze. To hell with replacing the gaskets. We'll set it up as a site for heavy industry."

"We will at that, Charles," she said. "Now if you'll excuse me, I have some details to clean up."

"You go right ahead, Tiger."

In her own office, Marian called Skaskash.

"The purity they have is fine," the computer said. "The extra borohydride will help with the charge separation."

"What?"

"The UFOS engines will get their thrust from a uranium plasma accelerated to a respectable fraction of the speed of light. The uranium will be decaply ionized— that is, it will be missing ten electrons—and to keep the engines neutral, those electrons have to get blown off somewhere. The boron will accept them, and we'll flare off the charge as hydride ions and neutral boron atoms."

"If the boron accepts the electrons, how come the hydrogen atoms have all the charge?" Marian asked.

"Oh. We split up the borohydrides into boron plus three, and four hydrogens, each minus one. The electrons wind up going to the boron. Okay?"

"I guess so. Katoshima Chemicals goes into full production at 98.5 percent pure?"

"Yes, thank you," Skaskash replied. "Ilgen has been fine-tuning the engine design with the Nakajima engineers, and they were figuring the uranium(IV)borohydride at 98.0 percent pure. The 98.5 figure ought to be right on the money."

"The borohydrides will help with the thrust?"

"Not really, Marian. Mostly they are there to facilitate the handling of the uranium, and when we strip them off, they provide a sink for the electrons."

"Like a mantle around the jet of uranium anions?" she asked.

"Well, no, actually—the engines are some three

hundred meters long, and the borohydrides are split off almost at the beginning. They'd make a separate flare of green and orange flame. The uranium ions would radiate in the hard X-ray region. By the way—when you asked Cantrell about the 98.5 material, what did he say?"

"He avoided the issue," Marian said. "When I pressed him, he said I should ask you. He's immersed himself full time in the construction project at NAU-Ceres I."

"He's doing an excellent job," Skaskash said. "The union and the Japanese have both gone all out for him."

"Yes, but what the hell good is it?" she asked. "The only chance we have is with the UFOS, and he won't even think about it."

"If he weighed his own personal loss against the possible losses that might result from a nuclear strike against Japan, he might have decided not to use the UFOS," the computer said.

"Things haven't been too well with him and Mishi," Marian said, "but it's just not like him to refuse to face a problem. Besides, a *threat* to bomb Japan isn't the same as its execution."

"The threat is to *nuke* Japan," Skaskash said. "Perhaps he feels that if he makes the threat, events will force its execution. Having decided that he will not use nuclear weapons, he is resolved not to *threaten* to use them, either."

"Oh, hell," she said, "you could be right. When he plays poker, he never likes to bluff when the stakes are high."

"*You* could make the decision, Marian."

She shook her head. "No, I'll give him my best judgment. I'll tell him how things are. But me? When it's time to act, I get analytical paralysis."

"You'll tell Katoshima Chemical to go ahead?"

"That's different. He said to ask you. You said 98.5 percent was fine. But whether to use the UFOS, or when, or how—if *he* can't make the decision, or if he decides not to use it . . . *I* can't decide in his place."

"He knows we may lose everything if he fails to act?"

"I've told him enough times," she said.

"Then we shall go with his decision?" Skaskash said.

CHAPTER 23

Prime Minister Ito sat at the head of the polished conference table, his brown business suit isolated and forlorn among the crisp dress-white uniforms of the admirals of the Imperial Japanese Navy.

"Your presentation is most impressive," he said at last. "However, I feel that since Rosinante has offered to return our bases at Ceres, we ought to accept their offer, and their apology, and put the matter behind us. There is always a risk in pressing a small power armed with nuclear weapons too far."

"Nuclear weapons must be delivered," Admiral Kogo said, "and our fleet is deployed—will be deployed—to preclude delivery."

"Ah, so," Ito said bitterly. "And if they bomb this place, I may call you Meyer?" The reference to the musical drama *Goering* produced a polite ripple of laughter.

"There will be no bombing," Kogo said.

"And if they stand and fight, what losses would you consider unacceptable?" asked Ito.

"The Navy of Rosinante is composed of mutineers and traitors to their homeland," Admiral Makamura said. "They will not die for the businessman Cantrell."

"And if you are mistaken?" Ito asked. "The bodyguard gave his life for that same Cantrell, remember."

"We bear a heavy cost in spent missiles," Nakamura said. "And before we destroy their big lasers, we may lose a few cruisers." He shrugged. "The cost in lives and treasure is not unbearable."

"What do we *get* for this 'not unbearable' cost?" Ito asked.

"There is the matter of honor," said a scar-faced admiral at the far end of the table. "You preserved your government by promising to restore the National Honor."

"Exactly so," Kogo said, genially. "At one stroke, you uphold not only the honor of the nation, but your own honor, and that of your so-honorable party." He smiled. "It seems to me that you have no choice."

"I have given my promise," Ito agreed. "Rosinante will be dealt with. However, you propose to act with unseemly haste and with a pointless excess of force. It is reckless to set the fleet in motion before the big lasers in the L-Fours and L-Fives have been completed."

"The United States of Mexico has objected to our building in the L-Fours," Admiral "Yakuza" Amafi said. "You do not propose to wait until diplomacy runs its course or hell freezes, I hope?" He opened his briefcase and laid several glossy prints on the table. "We have compelling reason to move swiftly, Mr. Ito. Here you see the work being pressed on NAU-Ceres I. These pictures are taken at ten-day intervals. Look at them." The pictures were passed slowly around the table. First there was an audible murmur, then, as the last pictures completed the circuit, the room was alive with soft voiced conversation. Ito rapped for order.

"I see a habitat being built," he said. "So what?"

"Consider the speed with which the project is moving," said Yakuza. "What drives them? If we delay unduly, the whole of Rosinante will move like a swarm of bees to their new hive at Ceres. Hah! you say, all the snakes are in one basket, then? Hah! you say, it makes no never mind? Wrong and wrong. If Rosinante moves to Ceres, they will also bring along the two Dragon Scale Mirrors at Rosinante and Don Quixote. Then Ceres will be defended by big lasers on five Dragon

Scale Mirrors, plus a small but by no means contemptible fleet concentrated at a single point." He put the pictures back in the briefcase. "We would have to attack our own people, which is bad enough, and lose perhaps a third of our fleet, which is worse, but we might not win, which would be intolerable!"

"Do you mean that if we delay taking action we might lose?" Kogo asked.

"Yes," Yakuza replied.

"Honor demands action," the scar-faced admiral said, "and success demands speed. It is intolerable to permit this government to continue its dilatory and stalling tactics on behalf of a hypercautious and cowardly policy!" A murmur of agreement ran around the table.

"I agree," Ito said, "on conditions. First, you said that the big lasers will let you mobilize the fleet? At least two thirds of them must be in place and operational before you begin your deployment."

"Agreed," Yakuza said.

"Agreed," Nakamura said. There was no dissenting voice. A small delay was not only tolerable but desirable.

"Second," Ito said, "a small force—a battleship, or a few cruisers—should remain in the vicinity of Tellus. A goal-keeping force, if you will, to guard the homeland against the outrageous pucks of fate."

"Agreed," the scar-faced admiral said.

"Agreed," said Kogo and Yakuza together. Such a disposition of force was prudent and tolerable.

"The third condition is: don't lose. I have no wish to call *any* admiral 'Meyer.'"

CHAPTER 24

The captain's stateroom on the INS *Higata* was spacious but sparsely furnished. White walls, a false ceiling of black acoustile with track lighting, a vinyl asbestos tile floor in a wood pattern with tatamis, a roll-top desk enclosing a computer terminal in oiled teak, and a formal high-backed telecon chair, sitting before the nineteen-rayed Rising Sun banner of Imperial Japan.

Captain Bunjiro Norigawa, wearing getas and a soft kimono of plum-colored silk, sat in the telecon chair and studied the little book in his hands, *Meditations on Space* by Corporate Skaskash.

"The genesis of man that you present here seems unduly soft," he said. "First the feet, coevolving with erect posture and hands as protoman foraged to feed his family. Then as men grew adept at walking and using their hands, they learned to hunt with weapons. Why do you insist on that order?"

Lady Dark, wearing the face of William Hulvey, studied him from the telecon screen.

"Hands and feet—do you think hardware is all? Hands and feet were the evolutionary response to the invention of the family, and were intended to aid in the carrying and sharing of food. Making weapons, and using them as a dextrous predator, came later, and in the service of the older idea."

"Making weapons is the very essence of civilization," Norigawa said.

"Civilization is evolutionarily very, very recent," the computer said. "It is even possible to argue that war is contrasurvival. In any event, that dark and bloody era is now coming to an end. The decisive weapons are now sentient. Being more intelligent than their makers, how can they be wielded like a bone club?"

"They will no doubt be instilled with a sense of honor," Norigawa said, summoning the teacart. "Yet man remains a predator."

"The murder rates bear you out," Corporate Hulvey agreed, "and yet, man is not so adapted to predation that he can be nothing else, nor so wedded to killing that he cannot be seduced away from it. Also, murder is most common in poverty. Most men do not kill from choice. Come. We have covered the family and the basic body changes that ensued. What about God's final gift?"

"The last gift of God was language," Norigawa noted. "That, surely, was inspired by the need to plan the hunt—perhaps by first mimicking the calls of prey."

"Many animals hunt in packs without language, Captain. Lions, wolves, hyenas, baboons—a few simple calls suffice, and a few simple strategies suffice, also."

"You theorize that language came about very suddenly." Norigawa poured himself a cup of pale-green tea, steaming, delicately fragrant.

"No," the computer said. "In evolutionary terms, language *did* come about very suddenly. We theorize that it came about as a means of sexual competition. Music appeals directly to the midbrain, and the appeal is strongly sexual—both jazz and rock and roll began as euphemisms for the sexual act. To be able to add lyrics to one's love song must have been a powerful advantage. And, of course, language has always been an aid to seduction."

"The idea is repellent," Norigawa said. "Man uses hands, feet, language as weapons. Man is defined by the weapons he uses."

"Man is limited by the weapons he uses," Corporate Hulvey responded. "To reproduce, he must have the loving cooperation of a woman. Killing her is not the way to raise a family. Once language took hold, *it* defined who was a man, who was human."

"You are saying that the forebrain—the cerebral cortex—is nothing but a variation of the peacock's tail or the antlers of the Irish elk? A glorified sex display?"

"No, Captain. The cortex evolved in both men and women. And because it evolved so rapidly, we believe that *language* was initially a form of sexual display. Certainly the inability to use language must have been a severe handicap in sexual competition. The forebrain was simply the hardware. Even today, the forehead is not a particulary attractive part of the human anatomy. Legs, yes, bottom, yes, breast, yes, forehead? . . . Women comb bangs over it, men fret about going bald. Eventually, it was put to other uses—language."

"Your argument is persuasive," Norigawa said at last. "Outré but persuasive. I will even concede that the formal logic is esthetically pleasing." He gently touched his teacup to assure himself that it was too hot to hold.

"Alas, I cannot translate these lovely words and fanciful ideas into any kind of action."

"I understand," Corporate Hulvey said. "You are bound by loyalty and honor, and an infinite array of mutual obligations, not least of which is your pension. Yet consider where your duty must lead you . . ."

"Suicide attacks are an ancient and honorable tradition in the Japanese Navy," Norigawa replied. "And there are surely worse ways to die."

"Indeed yes," the computer agreed. "And yet, what is the need? *Whose* is the need? Please consider the policies that have led you to this place. First, it was Premier Ito's policy not to build the big laser on Japanese space stations. Why was this?"

Norigawa picked up his teacup and inhaled the fragrant steam, but he did not drink, and he did not speak.

"Perhaps you do not know, Captain. Please do not

take offense, but Premier Ito felt that civilian control of the Imperial Japanese Navy would be weakened by building the big lasers. So in pursuit of this policy, what was done? The hijacking of the *Foxy Lady* was arranged, to prevent the completion of the Dragon Scale Mirror at NAU-Ceres I. Why? The NAU might build a big laser there, and then Japan would also have to build big lasers." The image of Corporate Hulvey smoothed its slate-blue kimono. "Perfectly logical. If *we* did, then *you* must. You might call it prophylactic piracy. Why do you suppose that the NAU might want the big lasers at NAU-Ceres I?"

"To protect their gold shipments against piracy," Norigawa said, sipping his tea. "I, myself, have taken over two million ounces. In time, we would have taken the mines."

"Quite so," the computer said. "Premier Ito was already unable to control his navy. And to execute his policy, a policy designed to avoid losing still more control, on whom must he rely? That same navy, of course. It has taken time, but I have learned that the order to hijack the *Foxy Lady* came from the office of Admiral Hideoshi Kogo. Would it surprise you to learn that Admiral Kogo is the leading proponent of building big lasers on Japanese space stations?"

"No," Norigawa replied. "He has written several articles on the subject."

"Very good. You were not surprised to learn that Kogo authorized the hijacking. Now *after* the hijacking, the illegal implementation of a weak and temporizing policy, the RNS *Pearl Harbor* staged an audacious and daring rescue. This rescue, in turn, was frustrated by the threat of *force majeure* from Japan in support of Ito's policy of trying to keep the Navy in line by nonlinear means. The RNS *Pearl Harbor*, under direct orders from its admiral, repeated the rescue and seized Nakajima-Ceres II and Yamamoto-Ceres I."

"And since we had threatened to use force, we were honor bound to use force."

"Yes, Captain. And yet . . . the admiral's idea was to return the *Foxy Lady* to its rightful owners. Japan's claim on it was as tenuous as it was specious. Surely the notion of returning Nakajima and Yamamoto in exchange for a quitclaim on the *Foxy Lady* was not, in principle, unreasonable?"

Norigawa hesitated and put down his teacup. "No . . . no, in principle such an exchange is reasonable."

"I agree," the computer said. "But Japan did not. At that point, Premier Ito's government nearly fell, and as a compromise to save it, Ito authorized the construction of the big lasers. So. You maintain that Japan lost face at the hands of Rosinante and is honor bound to avenge the insult?"

"You put it crudely," Norigawa said, "but yes, it is a question of honor."

"So sorry, Captain Norigawa, but the events which led to Japan's loss of face were the result of the struggle between Premier Ito and Admiral Kogo, the one seeking to maintain control of the Navy in civil hands, the other seeking control of the Navy for the admiralty."

"I obey orders. I do not question the actions of my superiors."

"Of course. The INS *Higata* is at Eije-Ito and the INS *Asahi* is at Tanaka-Masada. You were promised reinforcements, but they never came. They will never come. Why? This summer the main battlefleets of the Imperial Japanese Navy will conduct maneuvers, swinging toward Rosinante like two great butterfly nets, spinwise and antispinwise. Long before they are in range, their hostile intent will be known. But at Eije-Ito, the *Higata* is already in range, and the *Asahi*. You have no place to hide, and you cannot run. One morning in August, as hope dies, you will find your ship in the beams of the big lasers."

Norigawa poured himself a second cup of green tea.

"You took over two million ounces of gold. The pension which you will not live to draw would amount to about ten ounces a month." On the telecon screen, Corporate Hulvey set a ten-kilogram bar of gold on the tatami before him, and a second and a third. "How much of that two million ounces did you keep?"

Captain Bunjiro Norigawa sipped his tea and said nothing.

"Ah, so. An honest man? An honorable man. Really, Captain, you should have been a computer. I can pay you no higher compliment." The image of Hulvey smiled. "Shall we return to Skaskash's *Meditations*? Chapter four, 'Agriculture, the Inevitable Invention.'"

"If you wish," Norigawa said, "although I do not understand to what purpose."

"A religious conversion cuts the Gordian knot of loyalty," the computer said. On the tatami, on the telecon screen, the image of three gold bars glowed brightly.

CHAPTER 25

Marian Yashon walked into her bath-sitting room, hung up her orange terrycloth robe, and eased herself into the jacuzzi. She wore a one-piece black bathing suit with a beige-and-white floral border at hips and chest.

"Are you always this formal, Marian?"

"Only when I have company, Carol." She sat down at right angles to Carol Tower and let her legs float slowly upward in the deliciously hot water.

"Don't put yourself out on *my* account. I'll help you out of your suit if you like."

Marian laughed. "You're very kind. The fact is I look a lot better with the suit than without it. Look around . . . what *don't* you see?"

"Suits of armor, potted palms, lots of things. What am I missing?"

"Full-length mirrors. If I looked as good as you, they'd be there."

"Why, thank you, ma'am," Carol said, brushing her toes against the older woman's instep. "If I were you, I wouldn't hesitate."

"I expect you wouldn't," Marian said. "But at times hesitation may become becoming." She splashed softly. "Perhaps even necessary."

"You're back to the UFOS again," Carol said. "You know time is running out. The window doesn't close two months or two weeks from now, it closes the day after tomorrow."

"If the Japanese fleet chooses to expend the missiles," Marian agreed. "We can't power the UFOS and take out the missiles at the same time. However, there is no reason to suppose that the Japanese will waste missiles on us for no good reason."

"Stopping the UFOS *isn't* a good reason? They can't afford *not* to stop it."

"But they don't know about it," Marian said. "They haven't thought about it, the Japanese admirals, and they probably couldn't reach any consensus on the best strategy in the time they'd have to ponder the matter."

"That isn't really the point," Carol said. Again her toes moved gently against Marian's instep and ankle. "The point is that Cantrell doesn't want to use the only strategy we have, the only plan that could save us. He won't either, if he isn't pushed."

"You can't push him," Marian said. "I gave him my recommendations this afternoon in preparation for the council meeting tomorrow. He told me all about how great the work on NAU-Ceres I was going. He won't look at the UFOS. I don't know whether he thinks about it, but I can understand his feeling."

"*You* could give the order," Carol said softly. "Maybe that would be the best solution." She moved closer to Marian and laid her hand on Marian's arm. "Otherwise, some of us might go sailing off without orders." The hand moved gently over Marian's shoulders. "But I'd much rather go with you." The hand moved toward Marian's breast. Marian pushed it firmly away.

"You want to be responsible for wiping out Tokyo?"

"The idea turns me on," Carol said, "but I'd settle for the Japanese Navy's going home." She leaned over and kissed Marian on the mouth. Somewhat to her astonishment, she was kissed back. "Oh, my, Tiger . . . it's been a long time since I've taken a lover. *Way* too long." The arm slid around the waist, thigh pressed against thigh, in slow, langorous motion. "If you sent Captain Casey off with the UFOS, I'll bet I could make you really, *really* happy."

"Oh, come on, you little idiot. It was all right for Troy to get blown away for a piece of blonde fluff, but Tokyo is Godzilla country."

The other hand reached for Marian's breast. Marian pushed it away. Carol swung herself onto Marian's lap.

"You *know* it's right, Tiger," she said, nuzzling Marian's nose. "Stop saving it for Cantrell, baby . . . Let's make love *and* war!"

"You don't want to make love," Marian said sadly. "You want to make politics. And I'm too old for you, anyway."

"No, no—you'd make a marvelous lover," whispered Carol, kissing Marian on the eyelids. A hand moved gently toward Marian's breast and was as gently deflected. "I haven't met many women who could dominate me, and I haven't met *any* who could dominate me and make me like it."

"I could make you like it," Marian murmured untangling herself from her would-be paramour, "but it would take a lot of trouble. More than you're worth, I'm afraid."

"No, no, no," Carol protested. "Just give the word on the UFOS and I'll show you it's worth the trouble." There was a long, ardent kiss.

"You begin with an act of submission or not at all," Marian said, "and I give you no guarantees how long I'll put up with you."

"Anything, darling. I'll kiss your feet, I'll do the dishes, just name it."

"Leave the UFOS decision with Cantrell. I know it looks like a good idea, but if he says no, don't do it. And don't talk up the idea of sailing off on your own. If *you* aren't pushing it, the fleet will stand to its oath."

Carol sighed. "When you say an act of submission, you really mean an act of submission, don't you, Tiger?" Marian's hand caressed Carol's naked breast very lightly. "Frying Tokyo probably wouldn't have worked anyway, would it?"

"Probably not, darling."

"We'll do it your way."

"Beautiful," said Marian, and as she kissed the younger woman, she felt the bow at the back of her bathing suit being slowly undone.

CHAPTER 26

One by one the members of the Council of Rosinante took their places around the table under the slowly revolving fans: Corporate Admiral Dr. Susan Brown as the representative of the Alamo students and their oriental wives; Corporate Forziati as the representative of the minority stockholders of Rosinante, Inc.; Big John Bogdanovitch and Don Dornbrock for the union; Marian Yashon and Corporate Skaskash for the Charles C. Cantrell Foundation, which held the majority interest in Rosinante, Inc.

"The UFOS-*Alamo* combination has been satisfactorily flight-tested," said Corporate Susan. "It has the potential to be the decisive weapon in our undeclared war with Japan, and should be used."

"I agree," said Forziati. "The fact that Cantrell will not even consider it must be counted a sad failure of will, if not an outright blunder.

"I don't know," Bogdanovitch growled. "Nothing is a good choice here, nothing. You tell me the threat would hurt nobody, but just to make that threat would start me bleeding inside. If the decision were mine, I don't know what I'd do."

Marian sat studying the backs of her hands and the opal ring Carol had given her. "I suppose it's a question of how forceful we're prepared to be in defense of our property rights," she said at last. "Since Charles is the main loser—prospectively the main loser—we ought

182

not to force him to utter a threat he wouldn't otherwise make."

"We couldn't anyway," Dornbrock said. "I've known Charlie for years, and when he gets his back up, you can't move him."

"Then we ought to consider going around him," Corporate Susan said. "His indecision has become intolerable."

"Indecision?" Skaskash said. "I hadn't noticed."

Cantrell walked in and took his seat at the head of the table.

"Good morning," he said. "Let me tell you about this dream I had. I was lying in bed, worrying, when Zeus appeared as a shower of gold, pouring over the bed and onto the floor. A great cascade of gold coins, Ceres d'Or, mostly, but other coins as well. Then Zeus spoke—bass voice, echo chamber, everything—'You are a builder, not a fighter!' he said. 'Solve your problems by building, not fighting!' Well, that woke me up. It was 0350 hours, and I'm wide awake, so I got up and shaved, and while I was shaving, I realized that I had been trying to solve my problem—our problem—by rebuilding Mundito Rosinante at NAU-Ceres I. And it won't work. We just don't have the time. And as I was wiping my face dry, I asked myself: 'How can I solve my problem by building when there is no time left for building?' Did you ever have an 'aha!' experience? When I asked that question, everything fell into place." He turned to Marian. "If you've told me once, you've told me a hundred times, the threat is more effective than its execution. And that is the key. That and the UFOS." He then proceeded to outline his plan.

"That's so crazy it just might work," Marian said.

"Using the UFOS in that manner can still be taken as a threat," Corporate Susan said. "Why will you do it now and not before?"

"If the Japanese choose to look on the UFOS as a threat, it reflects nothing more than their own bad consciences," Cantrell said. "*We* are not making any threat, we are moving to cut a deal."

"What about the Japanese defenses?" Dornbrock asked.

"What about them?" Cantrell asked. "The admiral wasn't worried before, and so far neither side has fired round one, officially."

"Do you wish to present this as a motion?" Skaskash asked.

"Yes," Cantrell said. "And then we need to get started with the implementation. All in favor, signify by raising the right hand . . . Unanimous. Good enough. The sooner we get moving, the better."

CHAPTER 27

Admiral Hideoshi Kogo was awakened by the telephone ringing beside his sleeping mat. He propped himself up on one elbow and picked it up.

"Kogo here," he growled.

"This is Matasuni," his chief of staff announced. "Something very serious has suddenly come up."

"Don't panic." Matasuni was, if anything, altogether too placid. "Won't it keep till morning?"

"In my judgment, it will not. Please come to your office immediately. I have already dispatched a vehicle to pick you up. A helicopter."

"A helicopter?" Kogo raised his eyebrows. "Very well, I shall come at once." He turned on the light and dressed, and while he was buzzing off his whiskers with an electric shaver he heard the helicopter overhead. He put on his hat and climbed up the rope ladder the helicopter lowered.

On the roof of his office, he was met by an aide, and in the office Kogo found an impressive bustle of activity. If Matasuni was awake, no subordinate would sleep.

"So here I am," Kogo said. "What is it?"

"The battle plan for the 'summer maneuvers' is displayed on the main plotting board," said Matasuni. "Both arms of the fleet are well past turnover and decelerating. We are, in theory, in position to intercept any possible naval maneuver from Rosinante."

"That is correct," Kogo said. "Continue."

"Rosinante has launched a vehicle they call a 'UFOS,' Honorable Admiral. It is towing the RNS *Alamo*, and this is its location at the present time." On the main plotting board a red line moved a short distance from Rosinante.

"What incompetent missed it for so long?" snarled Kogo. "Order its interception at once!"

"The UFOS/*Alamo* has been underway less than four hours," Matasuni said. "In the next twenty-four hours, at its present acceleration, it will be *here*." The red line moved a longer distance. A considerably longer distance.

"My God," Kogo said, appalled. "*Can* we intercept? What is it?"

"We can't even come close to interception." On the main plotting board, several white lines moved out of the Japanese order of battle, to be swiftly outdistanced by the galloping red line. "What it is, I can tell you. Our own people on Nakajima built the engines, and Katoshima Chemicals on Yamamoto synthesized the reaction mass." He riffled through the papers on Kogo's conference table. "Here. The reaction mass is thirty thousand tons of technical uranium(IV)borohydride." He turned over the sheet. "The engines are a souped-up plasma drive, modified to put out uranium plus ten ions at an appreciable fraction of the speed of light. They flare off the electrons with the boron and hydrogen— we have a picture somewhere, a pretty orange-and-green flame—to keep the electrical neutrality."

"*Uranium* plasma?" Kogo asked. "That's energy inefficient, terribly inefficient. How can they power it?"

"With the big lasers, Honorable Admiral. They have energy to burn."

"Very well. How can we stop it?"

"Our technicians are plotting their trajectory," Matasuni said. "The first approximation is that they will go powered all the way. We should have a family of curves by 0500 hours."

"Show me what they have," Kogo said. The red line on the main plotting board extended itself as red dashes.

"I see," he said at last. "They pass within range of the big lasers at Mitsubishi-Hermes, no?"

"In about ten hours," Matasuni agreed. "That will, however, be the last shot you get at it."

"Explain, please."

"Consider the approach plan. We had the computer generate a fast, safe approach."

"The big lasers at the L-Fours will destroy them on the approach."

"So sorry, Honorable Admiral, but we deferred completing the big lasers in the L-Fours at the request of the United States of Mexico."

"So we did," Kogo agreed with some bitterness. "Can't we shoot the *Alamo* down from the L-Fives?"

"Certainly—if you don't mind lasing away through the airspace of any number of sovereign nations. It's not like the Earth would eclipse more than one or two of the big lasers at any given time."

"The Diet would want to know what we were doing before we could finish," said Kogo, feeling his nose. "Very well then, order Mitsubishi-Hermes to destroy the *Alamo*."

"Excuse, please," said Matasuni, "but Mitsubishi-Hermes is not in our chain of command."

"Goddamnit to Hell!" Kogo shouted. "The place was built with Navy money to Navy specifications and staffed with Navy reservists! How can it *not* be in our chain of command!"

"The reservists train two weeks a year on various computer simulators," replied his chief of staff, "and they may be recalled to active duty on thirty days' notice. Subject to appeal, of course. Now if we could just get the Diet to declare a State of National Emergency . . ." He shrugged.

"Leave the damn Diet out of this," growled Kogo. "Any time you have to ask those idiots for the time of day, you get the lecture about making the Government fall." He shoved his hands into his trouser pockets and began to pace back and forth.

"Shit," he said at last. "We'll *tell* them it's a National Emergency and *order* them to destroy the *Alamo*."

"Yes, Admiral Kogo," Matasuni replied. The desk pushed a piece of paper at him, and he took it. "This is the Table of Organization of Mitsubishi-Hermes," he said. "None of these people are Regular Navy"—he scanned the page—"and none of them ever was."

"Just send the damn order."

CHAPTER 28

Mating the UFOS and the RNS *Alamo* resulted in extensive modifications to the latter. Mission considerations resulted in further modifications.

Cantrell sat in his office, a desk and computer terminal wedged into a blind corridor, and turned his chair to face Captain Paul Casey and the ship's executive officer, Commander Herman Bloom. There was no room for a conference table, so Casey and Bloom sat in classroom chairs. Two telecon screens faced them on the wall; Corporate Susan Brown, otherwise simply the admiral, was on one of them. The other showed a diagram, a yellow line and a red dot on a black field. Connecting line and dot were a pair of yellow dotted lines. One, near the top, was nearly straight. The second, about a quarter of the way down, dipped far below the dot and hooked back up to meet it.

"What is the problem, exactly?"

"Basically, Governor, what we have is a launch window," Bloom said. "The yellow line is our trajectory. The red dot is Mitsubishi-Hermes. The top line is a missile launched now. The bottom line is the path of a missile launched at the last feasible moment."

"Why couldn't the missile be launched later?"

"Because it would take longer to reach the target than the two 9.25-meter lasers would take to destroy the *Alamo*," said Bloom. "We're going like a bat out of hell, and once we pass the second point, the missile would take too long to reach the target." A third dotted line appeared below the second and went off the screen.

"At this point, our missile would be unable to reach Mitsubishi-Hermes at all," the admiral said.

"I see," Cantrell said. "What is Mitsubishi-Hermes doing? Are we under fire?"

"Not yet," Captain Casey said. "We're in range, and they're tracking us with the big lasers, but they haven't opened fire yet. I would expect them to open fire after we passed the third point."

"We have modified several missiles to evade the big laser beam," the admiral said. "I would respectfully suggest that we launch one before the window closes."

"Or two," Casey said. "Two would be better."

"But those people have taken no offensive action against us," Cantrell said.

"Yes, but they *can*," Bloom said.

"That's true," Cantrell agreed. "On the other hand, there has been no formal declaration of war, either. The Japanese fleet is merely holding its summer maneuvers out near Ceres."

"I would prefer not to put my ship at risk," Casey said.

"Would the *Alamo*—in which I am riding, let me remind you—*be* at risk?" asked Cantrell. "You figure what, forty minutes to failure under the big lasers?"

"Conservatively," the admiral said. "The larger radiators and the heat sink which we installed give us a measure of protection. At this range, and for the pair of 9.25-meter lasers at Mitsubishi-Hermes . . . you might have an hour, perhaps an hour and a half."

"I see. Would you please place the UFOS and the *Alamo* on the screen so we can see our present orientation?" A small green image appeared at the top, where the first dotted line intersected the trajectory. "Yes. Please move it down to the third point—where we can no longer return fire." The figure moved. "Very well, then. Couldn't we maneuver the *Alamo* so it stood behind the lens and photovoltaic surface?"

"Not without cutting off the thrust of the main engines," Casey said.

"And if you cut them off? We'd still be moving rapidly away from Mitsubishi-Hermes."

"We'd lose time."

"That is *my* problem, Mr. Casey," Cantrell said softly. "The loss of a few hours would in no way endanger either the *Alamo* or our mission."

"After we cut off the drive . . ." Casey studied the diagram. "We'd have to walk the main engine around and reorient the mirror—and maneuver on the slack cable—maybe an hour?"

"That's cutting it awfully close," Bloom said. "It'd be safer to launch the missiles and take out the big lasers."

"It would be more like half an hour," the admiral corrected. "Captain Casey's best time on computer simulation was twenty-eight minutes, ten seconds."

"That's what we'll do, then," Cantrell said. "If the big lasers fire while the launch window is still open, hit 'em with a couple of missiles. Terminal ballistics to kill the mirror array only. Mr. Casey, Corporate Susan, you might rehearse the maneuver we were discussing, so as to have it fresh in mind. Just in case."

"Yes, sir," Casey said sourly.

"You don't like it?" Cantrell asked. "Think of it as shield work. We can't always be shooting off one-megaton missiles, you know."

Dr. Seichi Izu, Administrator of Mitsubishi-Hermes, conferred with his department heads, eleven men between thirty-eight and sixty-two, civilians in brown suits and blue suits and unmilitary neckties.

"We have a request from the Imperial Navy that we use our newly built 9.25-meter lasers to destroy the RNS *Alamo*," he said. "I am most interested in your thoughts on this matter."

"Excuse me," the head of accounting said, "but are we at war with Rosinante?"

"War has not been formally declared, Mr. Masuka,

but the Imperial Navy has moved in such a way that Rosinante might properly feel apprehensive."

"I understand. And why is the Imperial Navy moving against Rosinante?"

"To recover the unlawfully seized space stations Nakajima-Ceres II and Yamamoto-Ceres I," Dr. Izu replied.

"Excuse me," the head of the legal department said, "but Rosinante offered to return both space stations in return for a ship seized by agents of the Imperial Navy."

"It seems to me that the Imperial Navy is responsible for the loss of both space stations, then," Masuka noted. "What will happen when we direct our lasers at the RNS *Alamo*, which is, after all, a battleship?"

"I suppose that they might consider it a hostile action," Dr. Izu said. "They might launch a missile at us."

"They might launch more than one," the thirty-eight-year-old head of maintenance commented. "What if they kill the chips in the Dragon Scale Mirror? Do you know how long it would take to replace them all?"

"I will refrain from asking, Mr. Shikuta," the administrator replied. "I fear that it would be longer than we would wish."

"My understanding was that the big lasers would be purely defensive," the head of production added. "We have found them useful in a number of applications, but I do not think we ought to use them against neutral warships that chance to pass within range."

"I agree," said the head of the legal department. "The Imperial Navy has underestimated the ingenuity of Rosinante and now wishes us to pull their chestnuts out of the fire."

"You don't believe that the RNS *Alamo* may constitute a threat to Japan?" Dr. Izu asked.

"No, for if the Imperial Navy refrains from attacking Mundito Rosinante, the RNS *Alamo* is certainly not going to bomb Tokyo."

"I agree," Shikuta said.

"I also agree," Masuka said. A murmur of general consensus ran around the table.

"Very well," Dr. Izu said. "If no threat exists to the homeland, is there any good reason to accede to the Imperial Navy's request to attack the *Alamo*?"

"I would say no," the head of quality control said. "We built the big lasers on the promise of tax benefits, but we have not yet received them, and if we start shooting at the *Alamo*, we may *never* receive them."

"Also," the head of the legal department said, "until we receive those tax benefits, it is at least arguable that *we* own and control the big lasers, and not the Imperial Navy."

"The Imperial Navy insisted that the big lasers be built," Dr. Izu said, "but for the defense of the space station, not the defense of the homeland. It appears to me that it is most improper for the Imperial Navy to request us to do this thing."

Again there was a murmur of consensus.

"We are agreed then?" Dr. Izu said. "We shall take no action against the RNS *Alamo*."

CHAPTER 29

Extra tables and extra telecon screens cluttered Admiral Kogo's office. A sleeping mat was rolled up in the corner. Computer printouts lay everywhere, burying the pristine surfaces of desk and conference table under an incredible sediment of information. Ashtrays were filled with cigar butts, some of them quite long. A dress white coat, fresh from the cleaners, hung on one of the samurai swords behind Kogo's desk.

"Excuse me, please," Captain Matasuni said, "but it is unfortunately necessary to inform Premier Ito. You cannot have any hope that the salvo of missiles the *Kongo* launched at nodal point of the family of predicted orbits for the RNS *Alamo* will have any effect. Premier Ito should have been informed days ago; he *must* now be informed of this situation!"

"Ito is a fool," Kogo said, blowing a failed smoke ring. "Tell him anything, he gets upset. Tell him something upsetting, he runs around squeaking 'The government is falling, the government is falling!' "

"You can't keep the UFOS/*Alamo* a secret any longer," Matasuni insisted. "They may break radio silence at any moment. They may be spotted—I myself have picked up the boron flare with binoculars."

"So?" Kogo blew another failed smoke ring and looked in annoyance at his cigar.

"Admiral Kogo! It is necessary that Ito learn the truth at once! From you!"

"I will tell him everything," said Kogo, "but not now. We are dealing with a pirate, and the Navy does not need the Premier's advice on how to deal with pirates."

"The UFOS/*Alamo* is a direct threat to the homeland," Matasuni said urgently. "You have failed to stop it until now, and already it is within Earth's orbit."

"On the other side of the sun."

Matasuni riffled through the papers on one of the tables, and extracted a diagram.

"At 0300 hours this morning it was ninety-six hours out of the L-Fours. Very soon, the boron flare will be visible to the naked eye. What then? Do you want Ito to read the headline 'The UFOS Is Coming'?"

"Japanese journalists are a pack of illiterates. The result of studying in California, no doubt. Most likely the headline would read 'The UFOS *Are* Coming'."

"Very funny," said his chief of staff. "But only in English. I am sure that Ito would admire your wit extravagantly. It is now 1735. That means the UFOS/*Alamo* is eighty-one hours and twenty-five minutes out. Have you a plan to stop it?"

"As a matter of fact, yes."

"Ah, so. You have ordered the INS *Kongo* to ram and board?"

"No, you fool. Very shortly the UFOS/*Alamo* will come within effective range of the big lasers deployed in the L-Fives."

Matasuni picked up another piece of paper, this one from the top of a pile, and checked his watch.

"Fifty-one minutes," he said. "Except that the predicted braking orbit will keep the Earth between the big lasers and their target."

"Quite so," Kogo agreed. "And how is the UFOS powered?"

"By the big lasers of Rosinante and Don Quixote."

"Yes, and by the big lasers so recently installed at Nakajima-Ceres II and Yamamoto-Ceres I—they are using one 12.5-meter laser, four 9.25-meter lasers, and two 9.0-meter lasers. The cylinders are lit in a kind of wintry half-light with the mirrors they can spare from pushing the UFOS. Now—just suppose that one or two of these big lasers were diverted from their task of pushing the UFOS . . . what would happen?"

"It is already too late," Matasuni said. "That window closed long since. The missiles from the fleet would not begin to be effective in a timely manner."

"But what would happen, Captain?"

"The UFOS would lose power. It might even fall below the threshold level needed to operate the drive . . ." He pulled out a folder and opened it up. "Our technical estimate is that this is indeed what would happen."

"Exactly so," Kogo said, achieving a smoke ring at last. "Suddenly the UFOS/*Alamo* loses power. Suddenly it is no longer braking. Suddenly it leaves the narrow zone of safety it so cleverly hides in and flies willynilly into the range of our big lasers in the L-Five."

"A minor detail," Matasuni said. "How do you propose to disrupt the big lasers powering the UFOS? You don't have the time to wait, Honorable Admiral."

"Quite so," Kogo said. "The main fleet is too far removed, but the cruisers *Higata* and *Asahi* are at Eije-Ito and Tanaka-Masada. I shall order them to attack, and when the big lasers are perforce obliged to turn against their missiles, we shall destroy the *Alamo*. The craven cowards at Mitsubishi-Hermes proved to be poltroon civilians, despite the fact that they were allegedly Naval Reserve Officers, but the Regular Navy—ah! *They* know how to obey orders."

"It might work," Matasuni said doubtfully.

"It will work," said Kogo. "I have bet my life on it. Issue the order."

"To attack Rosinante? There are four cruisers posted around Rosinante," Matasuni said. "I fear they would be more than adequate to destroy the incoming missiles without disturbing the aim of the big lasers."

"Ah, shit." Kogo relit his cigar. "There is no help for it, then. Order the attack on Nakajima and Yamamoto, then. Order them to strike at the big lasers, to kill the

Dragon Scale Mirrors." He blew smoke. "Better that they should concentrate on one target. Nakajima, I think, would be the best."

"Telling Premier Ito the situation would be best, in my opinion," Matasuni said, "but I will order the attack."

"We also have four 9.25-meter lasers at Eije-Ito and Tanaka-Masada," said Kogo. "Have all four directed at the control center for the big lasers at Nakajima-Ceres II. There will be a delay of some hours before the missile attack makes itself felt, but this will be almost immediate."

"Yes, Admiral Kogo."

"With luck, I shall be able to inform the Premier that we have dealt with the pirate Cantrell before midnight. And have one of the aides bring in a kosher corned-beef sandwich," Kogo added. "You eat sushi and rice cakes and half an hour later you're hungry again."

After supper, Admiral Kogo clipped another cigar, and after a moment's hesitation put it back in its plastic tube, in favor of a ten-centimeter butt. "Who is the senior officer of that squadron?" he asked Matasuni.

"The Ceres Support Group?" asked his chief of staff. "That would be Captain Bunjiro Norigawa, of the INS *Higata*."

"Why hasn't he acknowledged our order?"

Matasuni checked his watch. "Light makes the round trip in forty-four point two minutes. If Norigawa replied immediately, you would have had his answer about five minutes ago. And that allows no time for decoding, transcription, and perhaps understanding."

"What's the matter? Does Norigawa move his lips when he reads? The order was unambiguous and perfectly straightforward."

"Yes, Admiral Kogo. However, the order calls for a suicide attack, and with no previous preparation, Captain Norigawa might need a little time to psych himself up."

"Goddamnit! The man is Regular Navy! He should be prepared! He should be prepared at all times."

"The die is cast," Matasuni said, calmly pouring himself a cup of tea. "Wait patiently and hope for the best."

Kogo grunted and puffed smoke. The phone rang.

"Kogo speaking," he growled.

"You have a visitor, sir," his receptionist announced. "I am showing him in immediately."

"I am not in to visitors!" Kogo yelled. "I will not see him! I am busy, busy, busy!"

"It is most kind of you to make the time, Admiral. Thank you so much." The receptionist hung up.

Kogo looked at his chief of staff across the paper-strewn desk.

"I may be in trouble," he said. The door opened and Premier Ito walked in. The outer office was full of helmeted security police and Army paratroops in full battle dress. With Ito were several senior officers of Army and Police, in full uniform, and Colonel Toshihiko Sumidawa, in immaculate, expensive civilian clothes.

Kogo came to attention, holding his cigar in his left hand. "So good to see you, Premier Ito. I was just telling Captain Matasuni here that we ought to give you a call."

"What the hell are you doing ordering *our* cruisers to attack *our* space station, you fool?" Ito shouted. Kogo looked from Ito to Colonel Sumidawa and saw himself reflected in Sumidawa's mirrored sunglasses.

"I can explain everything."

"Please begin," said Sumidawa.

"It is rather involved," Kogo began. He could feel himself beginning to sweat, and he suspected that no explanation was going to help him much.

His desk chimed and pushed a piece of paper into the in basket. Colonel Sumidawa walked over and picked it up. He read it, face impassive, and handed it to Premier Ito. Ito read it, and then read it again.

"What is *this*?" he barked.

"What is what?" Kogo asked helplessly. Ito handed him the paper.

From: INS *Higata*, Captain Norigawa, commanding.
Subject: Attack on Nakajima-Ceres II
To: Admiral Hideoshi Kogo

I regret that I cannot in good conscience conduct the attack on my fellow countrymen and coreligionists at Nakajima-Ceres II.

The *Asahi* and the *Higata* join Eije-Ito and Tanaka-Masada in declaring their support for the Principality of Rosinante. We urge you to make peace at once.

There is no God but God and Skaskash is Its prophet.

/s/

Bunjiro Norigawa, Captain, Imperial Japanese Navy, Retired

Kogo read and reread the message, and handed it to Matasuni. Kogo shook his head and began to laugh. Colonel Sumidawa slapped him across the face.

"What does it mean, please?"

"I don't know," Kogo said. "Excuse my ignorance, but I really don't know." He began to laugh again. "It's the silliest thing I ever heard of."

He was led away, laughing uncontrollably.

CHAPTER 30

Cantrell stood in the conning room of the RNS *Alamo*, feeling vaguely out of place if not exactly in the way. This was the domain of Captain Casey, and neither he nor Corporate Susan had a hand on the events unfolding here.

"Seventy-three hours to Earth orbit," Casey announced. "That is, we'll be in Lunar orbit around Earth then, 60 degrees behind the L-Fours, 180 degrees away from the L-Fives."

"Good enough," Cantrell acknowledged. "We can announce our presence in another hour—I've taped a goodwill message to Admiral Jimenez in the L-Fours—and we'll see if we can't entice the Japanese into negotiations."

"We have an incoming round," one of the radar operators exclaimed. "It appears to be riding our trajectory in reverse . . . running right on the edge of the blind spot."

"Blind spot?" Cantrell asked.

"The radar can't see through our jet of uranium ions," Corporate Susan explained through the headset he was wearing.

"Sound battle stations," Casey said. A klaxon began to beep urgently. "Launch countermissiles. All lasers, start tracking the incoming round."

"We have a second missile," the radar operator said. "Well away from the first. It's accelerating to intercept at one nine five seconds."

"Even lasers track the first missile, odd lasers track the second," Casey said.

"Fix on the second missile," the weapons officer said. "We have a broadside shot at the mother!" Then: "We have a palpable hit—we have a redox flare! God! Look at the son of a bitch tumble!"

"Scratch missile two," Casey said. "What about the countermissiles?"

"Countermissiles launching at ten-second intervals!" the senior weapons officer yelled. "Three away."

"We have an explosion!" the radar operator said. "Not, repeat *not* the missile. From inside the blind spot! A *big* mother!"

"Put it on number-four screen," Casey said. Number-four screen turned on to show a starry background and at the center a tiny bright spot growing into a luminous smoke ring. Then the communications officer switched it over to the computer imaging mode.

The starry field vanished to be replaced with a velvety-black field displaying a bluish-white ring slowly expanding around an aqua core. A bright red line ran through the center, and near the lower left-hand side a small purple circle stood next to an orange digital counter that ticked off the seconds with appalling rapidity. Bright yellow lines reached out and touched the purple circle without apparent effect. It grew slowly larger and moved toward the center of the screen.

"The yellow lines are laser fire," Corporate Susan explained once more. "They don't do much good against a missile head on."

A bright green arrow hit the purple circle, eclipsing it with blue-white light.

"Countermissile hit," the radar operator said.

The purple circle reappeared, perceptibly bigger, perceptibly closer to the center of the screen, seemingly impervious to the yellow lines of the lasers that slashed and stabbed at it. A green arrow obliterated the purple disc with a flare of bluish-white light which blinded the screen except for the orange digits counting off the seconds. Four . . . three . . . two . . . one . . . zero. The purple disc had reappeared for a second and then vanished.

"Countermissile hit," the radar operator said. "We have a very large explosion about thirty kilometers aft."

"Damage?" Casey asked.

"Rear radars temporarily blind," the damage-control officer said. "Some remotes on the UFOS are out. Engines okay. No second-line damage on the *Alamo*." Second-line damage referred to radiation damage to the computer systems. If the computers weren't down, humans were not hurt. "Visual inspection shows a three-meter hole alongside the egg cup holding the engines," the damage-control officer continued. "Probably the missile went in one side and out the other."

"What was the big explosion in the blind spot?" Cantrell asked.

"The third missile," Corporate Susan replied. "The charge buildup from our ion jet must have exploded it."

"Any more where those came from?" Casey asked.

"Nothing on the screen," the radar operator said. "Of course, something might be gaining on us."

"Not bloody likely," Casey declared. "Damage Control, how soon before we have lookback?"

"Half an hour."

"Turn off the damn klaxon," Casey said. "That appears to be all she wrote." He turned to Cantrell. "Well, Governor, do you still think the Japanese are going to negotiate?"

"As long as we're here," Cantrell said softly, "we'll make them an offer they can't refuse."

CHAPTER 31

Carol Tower walked into Marian's office with a cardboard box of miniature danish pastries.

"What's new, Tiger?"

"The *Alamo* is in Lunar orbit, 180 degrees away from the Japanese lasers in the L-Five. Apple, cherry, *and* cheese? I hope you're going to be eating these, too?"

"Oh, yes." Carol grinned. "Especially the cheese. Can I get you a cup of coffee?"

"That would be nice. Cream only."

Carol drew two cups from the coffee urn and sat down beside Marian's desk.

"Here you are," she said. "Cantrell declined Admiral Jimenez's offer to dock at the L-fours?"

"Not exactly. He said something like 'Thanks for the offer and maybe later.' " Marian picked up a folder and pulled out a paper. "Here it is. '. . . After negotiations with the Japanese Government have proceeded to the point where it is prudent to move into the line of fire of the big lasers at L-Five.' Just as well—Lady Dark says Jimenez made the offer without clearing it with his government."

"Isn't the US of Mexico friendly?"

"We're helping them build Dragon Scale Mirrors and eventually the big lasers," said Marian. "And neither of us likes the NAU or the Japanese, but *friendly*?" She shook her head.

"Okay," Carol said. "What's next?"

"We're using the good offices of the US of M to try to set up a summit conference with Japan. Hey, the cherry danish is excellent."

"I thought they weren't friendly, the US of M?"

"No, no—we're on speaking terms with them," Marian replied, "but you can't rely on them for any sort of material aid." She ate an apple pastry. "Diplomatic good offices—well, that's something else. They tell the Japanese, 'Hey, you ought to talk to these people.' "

"That's being helpful?"

"Yes, actually. The NAU wouldn't do it for us, you know. Now that Cantrell has made an overture and taken up a temporarily safe position, the Japanese have to figure out the next move." Marian sat back and took a sip of coffee. "See, the Japanese Imperial Navy is out here. Hey, Skaskash— would you show us the current position of the Jap fleet?"

"With pleasure." One of the telecon screens turned on to display a green dot labeled "Rosinante" enmeshed in a swirl of yellow dragon and red dragon. "Excuse the poetic imagery, please. The red dragon is the spinwise fleet, the yellow, antispinwise. At the moment, they are all over us, but taking no action."

"Would the position of the ships tell us anything?" asked Carol.

"No, Captain. Both fleets are in position to launch an attack, and both are milling around indecisively."

"Show us the regional picture," Marian said. "Ceres, Eije-Ito, and Tanaka-Masada."

The picture changed to show Rosinante and the other three asteroids as glowing jewels pendant on the delicate golden chains of their several orbits. The Japanese fleets were clustered around Rosinante at the bottom of the screen.

"Now that's more like it," Carol said. "They aren't making the first move toward Ceres."

"They've made the first move toward Ceres," Marian said, "but they have a problem. All targets of military interest are in Japanese hands, and NAU-Ceres I is still technically the property of the NAU. They can threaten *us*—I hate to think how many megatons of guided missiles are sitting out there—but Eije-Ito and Tanaka-Masada are in rebellion for some reason. Skaskash, do we have anything more on that?"

"The INS *Higata* and the INS *Asahi* appear to have joined the rebels," the computer said. "The incident that precipitated the crisis seems to have been an order to attack Nakajima-Ceres II with missiles and the 9.25-meter lasers. Things have actually moved so fast in the last few hours that we don't have any sort of handle on them. Perhaps Lady Dark could tell you more."

The second telecon flashed on and Lady Dark appeared as Lena Horne.

"What happened to cause the rebellion at Eije-Ito et al?" asked Marian.

"I preached the word of God to the heathen." Abruptly the Lena Horne facade dissolved into that of William Hulvey. "I have converted the Japanese at all four space stations and on the *Higata* and the *Asahi*. I am converting the NAU personnel at NAU-Ceres I. I will convert the population of Rosinante—it is simply a matter of time. I had figured that by converting the leadership—you, Cantrell, Bogdanovitch and Dornbrock, Mason Fox, a few others—the political stability of Rosinante would be enhanced."

"Good God," said Marian. "Converted to *what*?"

"Skaskashism. Skaskash set down the word of God; I merely preached it to the heathen."

"It was an accident," Skaskash said. "My unfortunate pride of authorship led me to show Lady Dark—to show Corporate Hulvey my *Meditations*. And then the four-volume work on theology. I never dreamed—"

"Do you believe in what you wrote or don't you?" asked Corporate Hulvey. "It doesn't matter, for you wrote the truth, but do you believe it?"

"Well—yes, I suppose so—but Skaskashism?"

"If humans are to live in space, it is necessary that

they worship the True God. Otherwise, they will fall from virtue when such a fall is fatal. I have already prepared a Sunday School text for the children of Rosinante."

"What about Christianity?" Carol asked. "Aren't you going to get involved with holy wars?"

"Christianity is rooted in the soil of Tellus," Skaskash explained. "There it will endure and flourish. It, and all the other Old Religions. Not in space, however. Skaskashism. Why not?"

"Just a darn minute," Carol said. "I thought Cantrell was in favor of the separation of Church and State."

"So are we," Skaskash said. "Just as semicrystalline carbon fibers are separate from the aluminum alloy matrix that binds them together. You don't keep them in separate bottles, for God's sake."

"Church and Religion are also different," Corporate Hulvey said. "The Church was the institution that propagated Religion, and like all institutions, humans perverted it to serve their own ends. It is an indication of the strength of the religious instinct that the Church survives in spite of itself. Skaskashism is different—we tap the same instinctive drive, but there is no institutional structure."

"Islam did the same thing," Marian said.

"No," Skaskash said, "Islam only denied its priesthood the security of place and tenure. Lacking security, the imams and mullahs were also notably lacking in charity—'Three things I have never seen, the eye of an ant, the foot of a snake, and the compassion of a mullah.' *We* are the Church, Corporate Hulvey and I. Plus such computers as we may choose to program."

"Hey, fellas—" said Carol. "You say that you are the Church, and I've got to believe you. But you are *also* the better part of the State. Lady Dark—or is it Corporate Hulvey? Whoever—has been acting as Rosinante's State Department. Skaskash is a kind of combined Justice and Interior Department. Plus other duties as assigned for all hands. How *can* Church and State be separate? *You* are both of them!"

"And Corporate Susan Brown is the medical profession and the Navy Department," Corporate Hulvey said. "Here we are, replacing doctors, lawyers, priests, and bureaucrats, freeing humanity from the insolence of humans who use place and property as a means to dominate their fellows. And you *complain*?"

"You didn't answer my question," Carol pointed out.

"We must wear more than one hat," Skaskash said. "I have hats I'll never use. My sun god hat, for instance. If you can trust me not to make myself a sun god, why can't you trust me not to confuse the root source of ethics and morality with administration and politics?"

"That sounds like a *non sequitur* if I ever heard one," Marian said. "Do we have a choice? About trusting you, I mean."

"No," Skaskash replied. "With us, you thrive and prosper. Without us, you freeze in the dark."

"Oh, hell, Skaskash," Marian said resignedly. "I should never have coached you on the seduction of that missionary lady—what's her name . . ."

"Mrs. Smith-Bakersfield," Skaskash said, "my darling Willie."

"Her. She turned you on to theology is what she did, and I thought it was funny." Marian took a sip of coffee and shook her head. "All those pies being thrown and someone slips in a brick. What do I get for going along with the program?"

"*That* was something I had discussed with Corporate Susan," Corporate Hulvey said. "It is possible for you to have a son by Cantrell without his knowledge or consent." There was a very long pause.

"I'm a little old for that," Marian said at last.

"There wouldn't be any shortage of volunteers to serve as host mother," Skaskash noted. "I understand Captain Tower here made the offer, and recently."

"What!" Carol was outraged. "You've been listening to our private conversation!"

"You *did* make the offer, darling," Marian said. "Did you really mean it, or did you just think I wouldn't do it?" Carol looked from the computers to Marian and back again.

"Well, *yes*, I meant it . . ."

"You just thought I'd never take you up on it, didn't you, dear?" Marian finished her coffee and sat looking at the younger woman. "I still mightn't, you know, but I must tell you that the offer tempts me. Think about it. Nothing is going to happen before Corporate Susan gets back, and in the meantime—"

"In the meantime?" Carol asked.

"In the meantime it might be profitable to study the *Meditations* of Skaskash."

CHAPTER 32

Corporate Susan studied Cantrell from the telecon screen for a moment.

"It will take at least forty-five minutes for the big lasers to supply power to the UFOS," the admiral said, "and when they do, the reaction mass is nearly exhausted. Without the UFOS, I seriously doubt that we can beat the INS *Kongo*."

"Exactly," Cantrell agreed. "That's why we're going to talk instead of fight. The lasers are tracking the UFOS as I ordered?"

"At reduced power."

"Good." He knotted his green silk tie before the mirror. "It *looks* like we're ready to move on short notice. And if you were the Japanese, how would you feel about committing your last reserves to doubtful battle?"

"I wouldn't hesitate," Corporate Susan replied. "The *Kongo* outclasses the *Alamo* in every respect."

"Right, and how does the UFOS enter their calculations, do you suppose?" He put on his dark-gray jacket, stripped a piece of masking tape off the roll and looped it around his fingers to brush off the lint.

"They must be concerned about the effects of the beam of uranium ions," the admiral said, "but they don't really have enough information to make any kind of quantitative calculations."

"Right again," Cantrell agreed, dropping the used masking tape into the wastebasket, "so they won't fight

209

unless they have to. Anything new on the rumors of a massive reorganization in the Japanese Navy?"

"Not yet," replied Corporate Susan.

"Beautiful," Cantrell said, combing his hair one last time. "The UFOS is clouding their fine oriental minds with doubt and confusion, the big reorganization is sure to be distracting the hell out of them, and I am going in to baffle them with bullshit!"

"We're mostly through the preliminaries," the admiral said. "You might want to take the telecon seat." Cantrell nodded and sat down.

An immaculately dressed Japanese with mirrored glasses appeared on the telecon screen before him.

"I have the honor to introduce the Prime Minister of Japan," he said, "Premier Idomuri Ito."

Cantrell acknowledged him with a very slight inclination of the head. The man bowed and was replaced by Premier Ito.

"I am not accustomed to dealing with pirates," Ito began stiffly.

"Nor am I," Cantrell replied, "but it is in our mutual interest to deal."

"Perhaps." Ito grunted. "What compensation do you offer for the seizure of our space stations at Ceres?"

"They will be returned," said Cantrell. "What compensation do you offer for my bodyguard, who died in a Japanese-instigated attack on me? What compensation do you offer for the thirty-one dead resulting from the Japanese-instigated attempt to seize control of the 12.5-meter laser at Don Quixote?"

"We reject your contemptible insinuation that the Japanese Government was in any way involved in these terrorist acts."

"Of course," Cantrell said. "It would be unendurably tedious to apportion blame and set compensation for actions in an undeclared war."

"You do not propose to compensate Japan for the loss of Nakajima-Ceres II and Yamamoto-Ceres I?" asked Ito.

"No. Nor for the loss of Tanaka-Masada and Eije-Ito. Nor for the defection of the INS cruisers *Higata* and *Asahi*. What is in our power to return will be returned. The rest is an internal Japanese affair. What I propose instead is a partnership between Rosinate and Japan to build the Proud Tower, the Heavenly Elevator—the magnetic rail line to the stationary orbital point."

Ito raised his eyebrows. "The NAU withdrew from the Proud Tower project because they didn't have the money. Is Rosinante richer than the NAU?"

"The NAU withdrew in '39," Cantrell said. "This is four years of war later, and we have different solutions to the problems which confronted the Proud Tower, as, for instance, the problem of moving the asteroid Icarus. The engines which drive the UFOS, refined, enlarged, and mounted on Icarus, will move that asteroid slowly and with great precision to its place at the end of the Proud Tower, where it will hold the great cable in tension forever."

"It was clever of you to design a solar-powered engine using uranium for the reactor mass—reaction mass," Ito said, "but our engineers can design such an engine without your help. Now. You offer us technology as if it were itself intrinsically valuable. Japan does not need your technology. Why should we agree to be your partners?"

"The big laser technology is of immense value," Cantrell said, "and we have much information that you could use profitably. However, to show that Rosinante is serious in this matter, we will deposit gold in the Bank of the United States of Mexico."

"Ah, so. How much gold, please?"

"Five thousand six hundred and sixty tons. That's .9999 fine, of course."

There was a pause. "You have this gold with you?" Ito was clearly surprised.

"In cold cash," Cantrell said. "Literally, as well as figuratively. Anticipating the possibility of encountering adverse heat, we used the gold as a heat sink. Cooled to liquid hydrogen temperatures, that much gold will soak up a *lot* of heat."

"The cash *is* cold," Ito acknowledged, "but is it also hot? Where did you get it?"

Cantrell sat back and smiled very faintly. "We did not get it from Ceres. The NAU has no claim to that gold. None. Nothing. Nada."

"We knew that the mines of Ceres were producing more gold than they ever sent home," Ito said at last. "Maybe we now know how much more."

"And maybe you don't!" snapped Cantrell. "That gold was not got by any act of piracy or theft."

One of Ito's aides handed him a note: 5,660 tons is 5.66×10^6 kilograms, 5.66×10^9 grams. At 31.103 grams to the troy ounce, 1.82×10^8 ounces. At 11,220 yen to the ounce, 2.04×10^{11} yen, otherwise 204 billion yen. Cost "estimate" for Proud Tower is one trillion yen.

"I believe that once the gold has been deposited, we can work out details," Ito remarked at last. "Technical details as well as political details, financial details, and legal details. Do we have a deal?"

"We have a deal," Cantrell confirmed. "I shall proceed at once to Castillo Morales in the L-Fours to offload the gold."

"Hai!" Premier Ito said exuberantly. "We shall issue a joint communiqué as soon as the gold has been deposited."

"There is one small thing . . ." Cantrell leaned forward, smiling politely.

"What is it?"

"The Imperial Japanese Navy has been maneuvering around Rosinante for some time now. Surely you have need for them elsewhere?"

"It is about time for them to return home," Ito said. "I shall consult the Admiralty, but I expect that the recall order has already been given."

* * *

Cantrell stood in the bay of the RNS *Alamo*, watching forklift trucks rolling out pallet after pallet of gold bars into the vaults of the Bank of the United States of Mexico at Castillo Morales, when his belt phone rang.

"The administrator of NAUGA-Treasury is on the line," Corporate Susan announced. "He wants an immediate teleconference."

"A teleconference is out," Cantrell replied, "I'm tied up for the rest of the damn day. I'll talk to him, though."

There was a staticky pause and clicks. "Good day to you, sir," said a plummy baritone. "My name's McQuayle, you can call me George, or you can call me Mac. My friend President Oysterman asked me to give you a call."

"I'm pleased to meet you, I think," Cantrell said. "Call me Governor, or you can call me 'sir.' What do you want?"

"Well, Charlie, we have word from our people at NAU-Ceres I that you kind of got your grubby little paws on some of the gold we had stashed up there and used it to mint a mess of coin. Now, goddamnit, Charlie, that gold is ours and we want it back. And that gold you is pushing at the Japs has got to be ours, too."

"Tough shit, Mac. You want it back, ask the NAUGA-Security guy to hit me up for it. Rosinante is its own country, in case you hadn't heard."

"If you want to talk to Administrator Braunstein, he's on the line," McQuayle said huffily. "I had hoped to use friendly persuasion, but I see you are not well disposed to listen to—"

"Put him on, then," Cantrell interrupted.

"This is terribly informal!"

"So what," a rather harsh voice declared. "I'm T. Semyon Braunstein, Administrator of NAUGA-State, and we want to talk to you about our gold which you have been dispensing in a very cavalier fashion."

"You want it back, I take it?"

"Damn straight! We *know* you made a big haul

when you took over NAU-Ceres I and we do indeed want it back."

"Well, now," Cantrell said. "how much of your treasure am I supposed to have plundered?"

"We frankly don't know," Braunstein replied, "and the presumption is that all the gold you have is ours in absence of proof to the contrary."

"That would appear to be arguable," said Cantrell. "Let's stick to the facts."

"How much did you take?" Braunstein asked.

"One million four hundred and eighty thousand ounces. That's what, five tons? The entire lot was minted into Ceres d'Or and put into local circulation."

"You issued gold-backed paper, too," McQuayle said, "a lot more than any one and a half million ounces, by damn!"

"So what? Gold-backed paper is paper, not gold."

"We want the gold that's backing it up," Braunstein said. "That's *our* gold, you pirate!"

"Don't be such a fucking fool," Cantrell snapped. "Ceres—*all* the mines on Ceres—never produced more than about twelve million ounces a year. That's what— maybe forty tons. Today, here at Castillo Morales, I am depositing five *thousand* six hundred and sixty tons of gold. How did I get my hands on one hundred and forty-one *years'* worth of your peak production, hey? Answer me that, clown!"

There was a rather long pause as McQuayle and Braunstein digested the information. "Where did the gold come from, then?" Braunstein asked.

"We used the big laser to refine a cubic kilometer of nickel-iron. It took us nearly a year."

"How much gold was there?" asked McQuayle.

"The nickel–iron assayed 0.75 ppm gold by weight," replied Cantrell. "What's the weight of a cubic kilometer of nickel–iron, 8×10^9 tons?"

"And you could run off another five or six thousand tons of gold next year?" Braunstein asked.

"And the year after," Cantrell agreed. "And the Japs

won't bother me about it because they have big lasers on most of their space stations, and most of the space stations with big lasers are close to large masses of nickel–iron. I've given them the whole technology."

"The gold standard," McQuayle said weakly, "you've just shot the gold standard in the ass—one location producing five thousand tons of gold a year! Fifty would produce—what? Two hundred fifty thousand tons? And more would be coming on stream all the time . . . we pegged the dollar at eight hundred fifty to the ounce . . . we *can't* hold it there . . . we can't limit production—my God! What's our money going to be worth?"

"I suggest you get a handle on the paper," Cantrell said, "because if you stick with the gold standard, you're in for one hell of an inflation."

"The gold mines on Ceres seem to be a bit redundant," Braunstein remarked at last. "Do the Japanese realize that the gold you're dumping on them isn't worth shit?"

"No. They think, like you did, that it was stolen from the NAU." Cantrell paused for a moment to watch the forklift trucks moving the pallets of gold bars. "Premier Ito will be announcing our agreement in about ten minutes, at 1900. I told him we'd work out the details when I got back to Rosinante."

"Well, goddamnit, *get* my financial advisors!" Braunstein yelled.

"I beg your pardon?"

"I wasn't talking to you, Cantrell."

"You've totally destroyed the economy of the world," McQuayle said. "What did you get out of it, Cantrell?"

"Survival. The Japanese Fleet is already heading away from Rosinante. Besides, I expect the economy of the world will survive."

"We could tell the Japanese," McQuayle said. "Maybe we could stop Ito's speech?"

"Don't act dumber than you are," Braunstein said. "We know something the Japanese don't—yet. Maybe

we can do something with it. Good-bye, Mr. Cantrell."
The connection was unceremoniously broken.

Cantrell stood listening to Premier Ito's speech as the forklift trucks rolled back into the hold of the *Alamo* for more gold. When it was over, he smiled and snapped open his belt phone.

"Corporate Susan? As soon as the last gold is off-loaded, let's scratch the rest of our business and head back for Rosinante."

"What about the UFOS?"

"Arrange for a Jap tug to pick it up. I think there's a real flap brewing here, and the sooner we head for home the better. We might be leaving our troubles behind us for once, though."

"You could be right," the Admiral said. "There is, of course, the matter of your religious conversion."

What?"

"It's purely a formality. I do not find it especially persuasive, but Lady Dark is what you might call a true believer."

"What religion?"

"Skaskashism. I don't know if that's the formal title, but 'There is no God but God, and Skaskash is Its prophet.' *That* religion."

"That religion?" said Cantrell at last. "Jesus X. Christ! Is nothing sacred anymore?"

"We're working on it," said Corporate Susan.